Two Tribes

FOOL'S GOLD

KRISTIAN PARKER

Fool's Gold
ISBN # 978-1-80250-516-0
©Copyright Kristian Parker 2023
Cover Art by Erin Dameron-Hill ©Copyright March 2023
Interior text design by Claire Siemaszkiewicz
Pride Publishing

Pride Publishing books by Kristian Parker

Speak Its Name
To Light a Fire
Call it Love
Spotlight on Love

Village Affairs
The Rule of Three
Three's Company
Triple Intent

Two Tribes
Fool's Gold

Collections
My Bloody Valentine: Venetian Valentine
Sun, Sea and Spotted Squid

FOOL'S GOLD

Dedication

To Nedra, thank you for all the support.
You have no idea how much it means.

Chapter One

Hi how are u?

Good thanks, u?

Good too :0)

I like your profile. You're a hot guy.

So are you? What brings you to Manchester?

Liam Moseley glanced out of the window of his small flat. The rain pelted down as usual, but no one expected anything different from summer in Manchester.

His phone buzzed again.

Here for work. You live here?

All my life. Can't you tell by the pale skin?

His flat might be a nondescript one-bedroom box, but he loved it. He'd made it as homely as he could. Growing up with a mother like his, he hadn't lived in any one place for very long, so it had meant the world to him when he could afford his own place.

A notification came through.

I think you're very attractive.

Thank you. Where are you from?

He put on his jacket. Harry would be here soon. They had some jobs to do today before heading to his boss, Jonny Wellingham's, house.

Buzz

Rome.

Must be a bit different to Manchester. What you doing here?

He needed to wrap this up before his day began. He'd only gone on the dating app to pass the time while he waited. Usually he would be on his PlayStation, but he didn't have time to get into that.

Searching for hot pale-skinned men? :0)

Usually on these apps, they got straight down to business, asking measurements and preferences. Having a bit of banter with someone made a nice change.

That your type then?

Putting his cigarettes, phone and keys into his pocket, he left the flat. Liam had always been a loner — he could feel out of place in a crowded room.

Out on the street, he wandered up to the main road. Harry would pick him up there. Time to put his game face on.

His phone vibrated in his pocket again.

It is now.

This guy was a joker.

Handy that. My type is fit Italians. But I've got to go to work now, sorry.

He liked to keep the parts of his life separate and wanted to get into the zone of being a Wellingham Boy. The Wellingham gang controlled Manchester. Gay boys were not welcome in that fake family. Jonny had made that abundantly clear over the years.

A black BMW came up the road and stopped right in front of him. The passenger door opened and Harry grinned at him. "You'll be picking up trade standing there. Get in."

Liam rolled his eyes and jumped into the car. As Jonny's right-hand man, Harry had seen it all. A Black man in his early forties, he'd been with Jonny probably longer than Liam had been alive. He'd had his fair share of problems over the years, but Jonny had protected him. Something that Liam respected.

Jonny might be able to scream at his boys for anything under the sun, but God help anyone else who did it.

"Where first?" Liam asked.

"The Hawaiian," Harry replied. "We need to pick some cash up."

The Hawaiian Paradise, one of Jonny's brothels, sat on the edge of the city centre. A rough old spot, most of Manchester had heard of it. Jonny hadn't spent any money on it in donkey's years. But he worked on the principle that horny men leaving pubs didn't really care about interior design.

Another message came in. Glancing at Harry, who seemed focused on the road, he slipped his phone out.

All work and no play. Don't you English think that is a bad thing?

He had a point.

I get plenty of play.

"Who's that?" Harry asked. "Some bird?"

Liam looked out of the window at the ring road. So many blocks of flats were being thrown up. Jonny had considered investing but had spent the cash on more stock to offload to the party crowd of Manchester instead. Jonny Wellingham only cared about profit.

"Something like that," he replied.

It felt quite cosmopolitan to be messaging someone from Rome. He'd barely left Manchester, but one day, when he'd saved up enough money, he dreamt of just taking off. His brother, Shaun, had done that and had the time of his life. But Shaun had ended up in Blackpool.

They drew up outside a kebab shop, a discreet sign above a doorway next to it the only indicator that customers had found their destination. It might not look like anything from the road, but it made Jonny an absolute packet. That, along with three other brothels and the fact that he had the drug supply of Manchester sewn up. He had done for years.

They got out of the car and went up the stairs to the top and the room that served as a waiting area. It contained a nervous-looking man in his early forties who stared at them in terror.

"Relax, sunshine," Harry said. "Just here to see the management."

Harry shook his head at Liam as they went through one of the doors that led off the main room to the space used as an office, staff room and store cupboard.

The manager of the place, Deb, sat at the desk, frowning at her computer. The frown dissolved into a grin when she saw them come in. "Who do we have here?" she said. "Dumb and Dumber. What can I do for you?"

Harry sat down on the old sofa. "Came for some cash," he said. "What else?"

Deb patted him on the arm. "You know, you could have anything you wanted. Mates' rates."

"I'll bear that in mind," Harry replied. "But today, we need to take Jonny some money. You know how much he loves it."

Deb sighed and got up. In her mid-thirties, she'd worked her way up to managing the Hawaiian. Liam had known her ever since he'd started running with Jonny a decade ago.

"And here's our cute little Liam," she said, pinching his cheek. "That baby face could make a woman want to corrupt it."

"Never mind all that," Harry said. "You've got a punter outside. He looks like he's about to scarper as well."

Deb shook her head. "Gina's taking too long with her current client. I've told her about letting them run on, but she's such a pro. Everyone comes for Gina, apparently."

Liam burst out laughing. "We should put that on the sign outside."

Deb produced a bag of notes from the safe under her desk. She handed it over to Harry, who regarded it with disdain.

"This is a bit fucking light, isn't it?" he asked.

"I know." Deb shrugged. "Business has been pretty shit. Don't be blaming me."

Harry put the bag inside his coat. "He won't be happy."

"Well, maybe if he spent some money on this place, he would get a better return." Deb sniffed. "Most of the rooms have damp and the mattresses... Well, let's not go into it."

It would be a brave man who would tell Jonny how to run his business. Liam left that to Harry. He had been on the receiving end of way too many screaming rants to stick his head above the parapet.

"Right, we're off," Harry said, getting up. "Can someone give that poor guy a fucking blowie in the next hour? We clearly can't afford to watch him leg it."

Deb huffed. "Fine. I'll do it myself."

"Where is everyone, anyway?" Harry asked. "It's like a bloody morgue in here."

"Not a clue, love," Deb said, checking her appearance in the dirty mirror on the wall. "Five of the girls have fucked off. They said they didn't want to work here no more."

They went out into the room. Luckily, the man still sat there.

"Right, sunshine," Deb said. "It's your lucky day. You got the boss."

"We'll leave you to it," Harry said.

Liam followed him down onto the street. A traffic warden circled his car.

"Don't even think about it," Harry said to him. "Wellingham business."

The traffic warden leapt away from the car as though it were about to explode at any second. "Oh…fine…don't do it again," he stammered before scuttling off down the street.

Harry shook his head, and they got in.

"Why do you think business is down?" Liam asked.

"Fuck knows," Harry replied. "But it'll be a bloody headache for us, no doubt."

They set off into the city centre. With Harry focusing on weaving through the traffic, Liam quickly checked his phone. He had another message.

Maybe we should play sometime?

The picture of this guy set all Liam's emotions running wild. In his early thirties, he had raven-black hair and olive skin. He wore his hair slicked back and stared into the camera as though he owned the world. That kind of arrogance made Liam weak at the knees.

Anytime

Harry's phone made them both jump as it rang. He had it linked to the in-car system, so the speakers kicked into life with *Simply the Best* by Tina Turner.

"Speak of the fucking devil," Harry said, clicking the Answer button. "What's up, Jon?"

"Who've you got with you?"

"Just our Liam."

"Right, I want you at the house now," Jonny said. His abrasive Mancunian accent always sounded like he was ready to lay into someone.

"What's up?"

"I'll tell you when you get here. Pick up Deano on your way."

The phone went dead.

"Sounds ominous," Liam said.

Harry sighed. He turned the car around and they sped off towards Salford where Deano lived. Liam hated Deano and Deano hated Liam. He had joined the gang a couple of years ago and made it perfectly clear he had no respect for anyone, including Jonny. He only wanted the cash and the excitement. *A dangerous combination.*

They got to his house in record time. A very handsome lad, he'd covered most of his body in tattoos in an attempt to come across as hard. His baby face always let him down so he'd created a personality far more ugly.

Deano got into the back of the car. His cheap aftershave made Liam and Harry gasp for air.

"Fucking hell, Deano," Harry complained, winding the window down. "You earn enough to buy something that wouldn't strip fucking paint."

"You don't know anything about style," Deano muttered. He swatted Liam on the head. "All right, gayboy? I bet you've got all the aftershaves at home."

Liam ignored him. Deano always called him that. At first, he'd denied it, but it only served to encourage Deano more, so now he just let it slide.

"The boss is in a shit mood," Harry said. "So if you could be a bit serious, I'm sure we'd all appreciate it."

Deano settled into his seat, sparking up a cigarette. "He's always in a shit mood."

"An even shitter mood," Liam piped up.

"What's his fucking problem this time?"

Harry shook his head. "No idea, but he wants us all there pronto."

"You'd better put your foot down then, Harold," Deano said.

Liam glanced at Harry. He had a scowl that would sour milk. They had spoken about Deano before and Harry had tried to get Jonny to bin him, but he worked hard and had absolutely no limits. Two things that Jonny Wellingham valued highly.

They carried on in silence. Liam sneaked a look at his phone. A message had come in from Marco.

Name the time and place. I'll be there.

He smiled to himself. It would have to wait until they dealt with whatever had got up Jonny's arse. But once he'd finished for the day, he might treat himself to meeting the handsome Italian.

What harm could it do?

Chapter Two

Thwack. The cue hit the snooker ball, and it went straight into the pocket.

"There's no beating you," Harry said.

"You have to rack them up again, then," Liam replied. "See if you can get lucky."

Harry sighed and emptied the pockets. The snooker balls rolled onto the table. Liam took a swig from his beer. They had been at Jonny's for half an hour, but he'd been yelling on his phone in the main house for the majority of that time. When Jonny was like this, the lads knew their place and headed into the pool house.

"I wouldn't want to be that poor bastard," Deano said.

He lazed on the sofa in his regular tracksuit bottoms and a Superdry T-shirt. All the lads except Harry wore those. Now over forty, Harry was significantly older than the rest. He absolutely refused to look scruffy. They might be well into the twenty-first century, but the police still liked any excuse to hassle a Black man.

"Deano, sit the fuck up. This isn't a dosshouse." Jonny came in through the patio doors and glared at Deano.

His rough way of speaking had no effect on Deano, who simply sighed and straightened up. "Everything all right, Jon?" he asked.

Jonny was more agitated than usual, if that were possible. He didn't have a reputation for being a reasonable man at the best of times. Sitting in one of the big leather armchairs by the fake fireplace, he looked up as if noticing Liam for the first time. Tiredness had etched itself across his face.

"Where are the others?" he asked, ignoring Deano.

"Next door. Getting their lunch," Harry replied before Liam could open his mouth.

Jonny lit a cigarette, exhaling loudly and running his hands through his receding hairline. He went mad if he caught any of the lads smoking in his precious pool house. He worried that his collection of signed Manchester United shirts would get contaminated. But he didn't mind sparking up himself.

"Jesus Christ, I'm running a bloody boys' club here," he complained.

"Do you want me to get them?" Harry asked. He placed a generous glass of whisky next to Jonny. He'd known Jonny since before he'd made his grab for power all those years ago and had a special way of dealing with him. Liam had learnt a long time ago when a situation called for Harry's touch.

Jonny's face shone bright red like a stop sign. For a man in his mid-fifties, it wasn't a good look. He took a swig from the glass and slammed the offending item down on the table. "No, leave them there for now. I need to get my head straight."

"What's going on?" Harry asked gently.

"Someone's dealing in town," Jonny announced.

Harry, Deano and Liam all stared at him, aghast. Jonny had had the Manchester drugs scene sewn up for nearly twenty years. No one dealt in the city without his say-so. A few had tried over the years, but they were no longer around. With canals weaving through the city like veins, there were plenty of places for enemies to come to a watery end.

"Are you fucking joking?" Harry asked.

"Because that would be really funny, wouldn't it?" Jonny replied. "I spoke to Baz at Below. They've been filled every night. All of them off their tits. And now you bring me some loose fucking change from the Hawaiian?"

Harry and Liam both jumped as Jonny threw his whisky glass across the room. It smashed against the wall, the contents running down the striped wallpaper that had cost three hundred pounds a roll.

"There's another gang. Has to be," Jonny snapped.

"What?" Liam said, stunned. "How can there be?"

The ashtray followed the glass, sending shards across the room. Liam stared straight ahead at Jonny. If he made any reaction to this outburst, he knew he would be on the receiving end of the next wave.

"I don't fucking know, do I?" Jonny snarled.

"Deano. Get him another drink," Harry said.

Deano went over to the mirrored bar and set about making Jonny's whisky and splash of water. Harry sat down next to Jonny. Liam stayed rooted to the spot.

"Tell us," Harry said, soothingly.

Jonny focused on Harry's face. He seemed lost there for a second. Liam had never seen him like that before.

"Bastards are dealing in Below, in Rylands and in the frigging Student Union," Jonny muttered.

Deano made an exclamation. "Shit, boss."

Jonny accepted the drink and downed it one before standing up. He paced up and down the room with everyone watching him. He had been a force to be reckoned years ago, but now he got others to do his dirty work. *The natural succession in the world of gangs.*

"I've had this city for twenty fucking years," Jonny ranted. "I'm not just bending over for some twat who thinks he can make a name for himself."

"We should find out who it is and finish them," Liam suggested.

Jonny whirled on him, his face getting so close Liam could smell the stale whisky and cigarettes on his breath. "Well, thank you for that input, brains. I wouldn't have thought of that, would I?"

Flecks of spittle decorated Liam's face, but he stood his ground. To cower away would only anger Jonny more. Liam didn't fancy a snooker cue smashing over his head.

Instead, he employed his usual method. He counted to twenty in his head until the storm passed. Jonny had only properly hurt Liam once. Years ago, Liam had lost a grand's worth of cocaine. It had fallen out of his backpack as he'd cycled down the canal to meet one of Jonny's dealers. To be fair, Jonny had been sorry and sent a Nintendo Switch to the hospital.

"You fucking leeches hang around this house like shit on my shoe," he ranted. "I do the thinking, all right? If I left it to you thick bastards, we'd have lost everything years ago."

He shoved Liam out of his way and carried on pacing. Shame stung Liam's cheeks as he knew Deano would be staring, but he kept his head down.

"What are you going to do, boss?" Harry ventured.

"I don't know, do I?" Jonny spat back.

"Is Baz going to sort it?" Deano asked.

Jonny grabbed a snooker ball from the table and threw it at him. He ducked out of the way, but it smashed into Jonny's framed picture of him with Liam Gallagher.

"He reckons he can't control the dancefloor, and that's where they're dealing. He's even reviewed the fucking CCTV and can't work out who it is. The snide bastard. I bet he's getting a cut from them. I'll show him."

He stalked across the room before stopping at the door. "Has anyone heard from Dave?"

Dave worked as Jonny's main dealer in town and had gone worryingly quiet over the last few days. They all shook their heads.

"If he rings, come and get me. Anything else, leave me fucking be."

The door slammed as Jonny went into the main house. The lads were rarely allowed in there. Occasionally at Christmas, although it felt weird and most of them preferred their little den. Jonny had built the pool house as an annex to house the lads.

The building had been a vanity project with a small kitchen and bathroom. It even had most of the drugs they distributed around Manchester in the loft, along with a little dormitory in case lads needed to stay over. Every room had pictures of Jonny in them. Jonny's boys could never forget who paid their wages.

As silence descended on the room, they all exhaled at the same time.

"Shit," Deano said.

Harry got up and put his hand on Liam's shoulder. "You all right, lad?"

He couldn't show any weakness. Not in front of Deano. He homed in on that like a great white shark.

"Course I am," Liam said, summoning bravery nobody believed. "Water off a duck's back."

"He speaks to you like shit," Deano sneered. "You shouldn't stand for it."

"I didn't see you piping up when you nearly got a snooker ball in your mush," Harry said. "Shut the fuck up."

Liam started to put the balls tidily on the table, ignoring the scornful stare from Deano.

"See, he has to get you to fight his battles. Soft as shit," Deano teased.

Putting the triangle down, Liam set off to the patio door. "I'm going for a smoke."

He walked out with Deano's cackles ringing in his ears. Lighting a cigarette, he leant against the wall and closed his eyes. The sunlight on his face made a welcome change. Manchester wasn't known for its sunshine but the rain of that morning had long gone.

"They taking the piss out of you?"

Liam blinked in the sunlight before seeing Sadie Wellingham, Jonny's twenty-year-old daughter, standing next to him.

"When are they never not taking the piss?" he replied.

A chip off the old block, Sadie wasn't attractive, but she made the most of what she had with her red hair piled up on her head and heavy makeup that she never left the house without. She took the cigarette from his fingers.

"If your dad sees you, I'll get it in the neck," Liam said.

Taking a drag, she handed it back to him. "Then don't let him see. You need to toughen up, Liam. Have you never asked yourself why Deano is getting all the good jobs? He's only been here two years. You've been here bloody ten."

He had asked himself that question many times over the last few years. Deano got the best wheels and led on things. Liam usually ended up keeping watch.

"No ambition," Sadie continued. "My father needs lads that can think for themselves."

"You're an expert in running a gang now, are you?"

When Liam had first joined Wellingham's, Sadie had been a cheeky ten year old. Now a grown woman, a serious attitude problem had replaced the cheek. Jonny had insisted she go to university to study business. One day, she would be quite the catch. Not that any of the lads would dare do anything about it. Jonny would have them strung up. It would be a brave man who dated Sadie Wellingham.

"This new gang. What do you know?" she continued, ignoring his question.

"You should ask your dad about that."

"Pah," she said, taking the cigarette from him again. "He won't tell me shit. Says it's no place for a woman."

"Maybe he's right."

Scowling, she dropped the cigarette and ground it under her shoe.

"Hey, there were loads left on that," he protested.

With a haughty expression, she looked him up and down. "You're nearly thirty, Liam. You say there's no place for a woman? More like no place for a sad bastard in trackies."

She didn't wait for a response and stalked round the side of the building. Liam caught sight of himself in the window.

He saw himself through her eyes. Jonny's lads were usually in their early twenties. Most had moved on by the time they got to Liam's age.

What did she know, anyway? Liam was loyal and the fact was, he had nowhere else to go.

"Rotten bitch," he said to himself as he wandered back inside.

Chapter Three

The streets of the city centre were quiet. It was that strange lull time between commuters dashing home to spend yet another night in front of the television and the party crowd who were ready to drink the bars dry. Then Jonny's lads' phones would be ringing.

Manchester had always had a reputation as a party city. Jonny often regaled them with stories of the nineties when local bands like the Happy Mondays and Oasis ruled the charts. Jonny had cut his teeth dealing to the acid house crowd who flooded the world-famous Hacienda nightclub…before it all went wrong. The club might be a distant memory, but its legacy lived on.

Liam walked across the eyesore known as Piccadilly Gardens, a spot full of cheap druggies and petty criminals. Jonny refused to deal directly to them. He thought it tainted his business. He didn't mind others doing it for him though.

Very early on, Jonny had aimed higher. Once he'd got rid of his old boss, he had set up supply lines into the city that ensured they never ran out of stock to sell to an ever-increasing market. By the time Liam had joined him, the big money rolled in on a daily basis.

Liam walked past the fancy bars of the Northern Quarter. Housed in the old buildings of Manchester's past industrial era, these were the haunts of the media, the computer whiz kids and the marketing executives. Jonny liked to have his boys deal sell their produce directly on this patch, instead of going through the dealers. Career-driven customers didn't take unnecessary risks and always had cash. Jonny's product would be all over this district tonight.

But Liam wasn't selling that night. He carried on walking until he reached the Mayfield Arms. Nestled on a tiny side street, this ancient watering hole had survived the hard times of the twentieth century and the gentrification of the twenty-first.

Inside, the crowd of people seemed to be on another planet from the champagne-and-cocaine crowd packing the watering holes which surrounded it. Liam nodded to Mel behind the bar. She had been there since before he could remember.

"Usual, Liam love?" she shouted above the din.

"Yeah. Is she in?"

Mel nodded to the other room.

"Better get her a gin then," Liam said with a wink.

Mel bustled about getting his order. Liam nodded in acknowledgement to a couple of the old customers.

"Not working tonight then, Liam?" Patrick, a man who looked older than time but was probably only in his sixties, asked.

"Nah, footloose and fancy free, Pat."

"I don't know why you bother with this shithole. A young lad like you should be down the Locks. Get yourself a bit of skirt."

Mel slammed his pint down on the bar. "Less of the shithole, thank you. You've been coming here for twenty bloody years. Gin and tonic as well, love?"

Liam nodded. "I'd rather be in here than down that bloody meat market."

Taking a swig of his pint, he glanced around. He could have a proper night off in here. They operated a strict drug-free zone, and Liam enjoyed that. Most people around town knew Liam as one of Jonny's lads. They were always hassling him for gear. Besides, trying to cop off with girls down Deansgate Locks would never appeal.

"You're an old man in a young man's body, you," Patrick muttered.

"Nothing wrong with that," Liam countered.

Patrick shook his head. "You won't be saying that when you *are* an old man. It doesn't work the other way around, you know, lad. Your mother knew how to live life. She got thrown out of this place more times than I've hot dinners."

Most of the locals could tell a story or two about his mum, which also kept him coming back. He had heard them all a thousand times, but it didn't matter. Somehow it made him feel close to her, even for a split second.

"Twelve pound sixty," Mel said as she brought the gin over.

Liam gave her a twenty-pound note and picked the drinks up. "Get one for Pat," he replied.

"You're a good lad," Patrick said with a smile.

Liam fought his way through the crowd to the little room off the bar. As usual, the punters didn't bother with this room and the tables in the corner were fairly empty. They had an unwritten rule that these were reserved for the working girls. For decades they had come to the Mayfield to fortify themselves before a shift pleasing their punters.

In the corner sat his best friend, Claire Lucas. Five-foot-four, with raven-black hair and a perfect hourglass figure, Claire had long been one of the most successful sex workers in Jonny's houses. Even past the critical age of thirty, she still brought in more money than three of her rivals who shared space with her.

"Hey up, it's our Liam," she shouted across the room.

A sea of people milling around opened up. Claire had a voice that could curdle milk. He sat down next to her and handed her the gin.

"And he comes bearing gifts. You can stay." She planted a kiss on his cheek.

"How have you been? It's been bloody mad this week," Liam said. He took a long swig of his pint. God, it tasted good. He had been known to dabble in other things, but a decent pint of lager was difficult to beat.

Claire turned away from the girls she had been chatting to. "I need to talk to you," she said, lowering her voice.

"What's up?"

She took a swig of her drink and glanced around. The other customers were deep in conversation, but she still huddled closer to him. "Gina and Deb have had a call. A weird one."

Liam pulled a face. "Nothing new, is it?"

"Not a punter. A foreign-sounding fella. He wanted to meet up with them. All hush-hush, like."

Liam could see his night off disappearing before his eyes. Did he really want Claire to tell him something he would have to take to Jonny? "What, like a hotel or something?"

Jonny ran his brothels with a strict code. They didn't meet clients anywhere but in-house. If he got wind they were moonlighting, there would be hell to pay. Although losing five girls in a week probably meant that Jonny couldn't afford to be too harsh.

Claire shook her head. "I told you, he's not a punter. They didn't go in the end. But…"

She had guilt written all over her face. Liam smelt a rat. "But you did?"

Claire nodded.

"Fucking hell, Claire."

"Don't get out of your pram. I only wanted to see."

Liam took a bigger swig of his drink. "Well, spit it out then."

Absentmindedly picking at her chipped nail polish, she avoided his eyes. *Never a good sign.* "Now listen to what I have to say before you go off on one. Brave bastard is setting up a new operation. Right under Jonny's nose."

"Claire—"

"Hear me out I said. He's going to run pop-up houses."

Liam frowned. "What the fuck are they?"

"He rents an apartment for the weekend. Real nice ones. We work from it. Then boom, we disappear. Next time it's somewhere different."

Liam thought it over. It sounded like a good idea. In the last five years, Manchester had filled up with apartments for nightly rents. Hen parties and stag dos liked the space and were less likely to get thrown out for noise than in a hotel. It would work brilliantly as a temporary base. The amount Jonny spent on keeping his brothels out of the limelight made Liam shudder. What he could do with that money…

"It's better than being in some grimy dump stinking of kebabs," Claire continued. "The punters get the address then and there. Job done."

It bothered him that Claire had done this though. Everyone knew he and Claire were best mates. "You need to stay away from this. Some bastard is dealing around town."

Claire's eyes widened. "Fuck me. He's got balls of steel, this one."

Liam didn't like the shine of admiration in her eyes. "I mean it. You can't get involved."

"He's offering ten percent more than that bald bastard. Plus, he said he'll put proper security on. You saw Darlene last week. That guy messed her up bad, and with no lads in the place, what the fuck are we supposed to do?"

"Jonny said he'd put Steve and Aleck on this weekend."

Claire laughed. "Give me a break. Those two couldn't knock the skin off custard."

If she left Jonny's employ, Liam would probably be banned from seeing her. The thought struck fear in his heart. He didn't open up to many people, but Claire knew everything about him. To lose her would be devastating.

"Are you moving, then?" he ventured.

"I'm tempted, Li. I can't lie. A lot of the girls have already gone," she whispered. "Word is that Wellingham's finished. There's only Moira and Jilly in the Paradise Rooms now. If Gina and Deb go, he'll have lost nearly half his girls. If it's the same guy who's fucking up his dealing as well, what does he have left?"

Liam squeezed the bridge of his nose. His eyes were aching like crazy. It had been a hell of a day and a quiet drink with Claire before she started work had turned into another headache.

"I'll have to tell him," Liam said. "I won't mention names, but if he knows I know —"

Claire grabbed of his arm and leant closer. "This is your chance to get out, babe. You could do security for this new guy or deal a bit. Make some decent cash. We could get a place in town. You can't like living in that shithole."

He thought about his one-bedroomed flat. He'd been proud as Punch when he'd rented it. Before that, he'd sofa surfed and Harry had put him up for a bit. But he could only afford a dodgy area south of the city centre. Jonny lived in the suburbs and he liked his lads close, but not too close.

Liam made decent money with Jonny, but flats in town were seriously expensive. Liam and Claire had always dreamt of getting a pad with a view. But dreams didn't come true that easily.

"And what the fuck would I do when Jonny and the lads come knocking? He isn't going to pat me on the back and say, 'Fair enough, lad. I've lost it, on you go.'"

Claire took a large swig of her drink. "You can't be Jonny's lapdog forever. You're twenty-six. Don't you want more out of life?"

She couldn't or wouldn't understand his priorities. "You know I can't leave him. Not just because he'd rip my bollocks off. What if Mum came home?"

Pity crossed her face, which made him want to throw up. "It's been ten years, babe. You haven't heard a thing from her. She isn't coming back."

Unable to meet her gaze, he also drained his glass. "She's coming back, Claire. I know she is."

"And in the meantime, you're going to throw your life away on that piece of shit? This is the best opportunity you've ever had. Don't be a dick."

He'd had enough of her going on. He knew that when Claire got something in her head, she was like a runaway train. After listening to Jonny ranting all day, Liam didn't need it.

"Save your stroppy response," Claire said, gathering up her things. "It's nearly ten. I've got to get to work. Think about it though, yeah?"

He nodded sullenly. He didn't like falling out with her. She kissed him on the cheek.

"When did you last have a day off or a decent night out or even a bloody shag, for God's sake? You're giving him too much, Li." With that, she set off to work, pushing her way through the drinkers, her short stature making her disappear in no time. Liam watched her go.

To his surprise, Mel put a fresh pint down in front of him. "On the house, love. Pay no heed to her. Was she giving you a hard time?"

Liam picked up his glass. "Thanks, Mel. Nothing I can't handle. You know Claire."

"I certainly do. She thinks she knows everything, that one."

Mel set about collecting empty glasses from the tables. She knew Claire almost as well as he did. Claire did think she had the whole world sussed. But maybe she'd got it right about some things.

He got his phone out of his pocket and fired it up. He would show her.

Chapter Four

How r u today?

Liam had switched his notifications off, but his phone still vibrated on the pub table. He had moved on from the Mayfield to a trendier spot. BARb sat on Livingstone Square, closer to the centre of town.

It was the same guy from earlier. Liam's stomach did a little dance. He checked the profile of the person messaging him. He had some serious good looks, with tan skin and dark hair. He hadn't been able to get him out of his head since their chat the day before. Liam had a rule—he never went near anyone from Manchester. He needed to keep this as discreet as possible. This guy was from bloody Rome. *Perfect.*

Good thanks, u?

He took in the crowd of the small bar that had dance music thumping. No one paid him any attention. After he'd finished his pint in the Mayfield, he'd had an idea.

What if he could catch one of their old dealers in the act? BARb was a known drugs hang-out. He should know — he'd made enough money there in his time.

His phone vibrated again.

Are you working or playing tonight?

He stared at the picture on the profile again. This guy was drop-dead gorgeous. After what Claire had said, he vowed to prove her wrong. With a swig of the weak beer they served here, he took a deep breath.

Playing

Now he would probably never hear from the guy again. Some men, alone in hotel rooms, just relished the chase and a bit of flirty banter. Liam knew he wasn't a bad-looking guy, but he also knew when someone was out of his league.

To his astonishment, his phone buzzed.

Well, handsome guy. Fancy meeting a stranger in your city for a drink?

This wasn't the usual response. He generally got invited to a hotel room for an hour of fun with a visiting businessman. The idea of meeting someone for a drink stepped over the boundaries that Liam had set for himself.

Just as he went to press Block, Claire's words echoed in his mind. He did want more out of life than being Jonny Wellingham's lapdog. He could meet someone for a drink without having to explain himself. Without thinking, he hastily replied.

OK. Meet me at St Peter's Square at seven. Outside the library.

He pressed Send and tried to ignore his heart hammering away. People did this sort of thing all the time.

* * * *

A quarter of an hour later and his heart rate hadn't died down. If anything, it had sped up. He stood outside the library, watching every person passing by in case he recognised them. But they were just people going about their business on the warm August evening.

The nerves were whirling around his body. He kept thinking of Claire and how she was always badgering him to try to find a decent guy. How could he? As soon as he told them how he made a living they would go. They all went eventually. His mother, his brother, everyone.

He glanced at his watch. It had gone seven now. He should have known a handsome Italian guy would get a better offer in that time.

Taking one last look around, he set off the way he had come, towards his favourite bars. His original plan of getting obliterated still stood and there were countless places that would help him on his mission.

"Hey there," a thickly accented voice shouted.

Stopping and turning, Liam found his breath catching in his throat when a gorgeous man sprinted towards him. Shorter than he'd imagined, he looked even better in the flesh if that were possible. He had jet-black hair gelled into a quiff—a look that made Liam go weak at the knees. Add that to gorgeous tan skin and a smile that burst over his face and Liam half expected him to say there had been a mistake, that Liam didn't look like his profile picture and that would be that.

"Sorry I'm late," the man said as he caught up with Liam. "Marco."

He thrust out his hand, which Liam took. "Liam," he replied.

"I got my squares mixed up," Marco said. His smile lit up his whole face and Liam could spend all evening just staring into his almond-shaped dark brown eyes.

"Not to worry," Liam replied. He hated when he got shy, but this guy had him totally out of his depth now that they stood facing each other.

"Well? Fancy that drink?" Marco said, seemingly oblivious to Liam's discomfort.

Liam nodded. On his way over, he had been wracking his brains for where to go. He absolutely wouldn't go to the Gay Village, a few streets away. That would be flying way too close to the wind. In the end, he had settled on Best's, a sports bar near the town hall.

They walked along the pavement. Liam could hardly look at this guy. He was so handsome it made him uncomfortable. The scent of his cologne was citrussy and seriously expensive, much better than the drain-cleaner shite Deano had turned up in. Marco seemed perfectly content to walk in silence. He exuded confidence.

"Where are you staying?" Liam managed eventually.

"I'm at the Radisson just down there," Marco replied.

Liam whistled. "Very posh."

Marco laughed. A free and infectious laugh. "That's me. Italian royalty, you know."

Liam finally glanced at him. "Really?"

Marco shook his head. "Sadly not. But my uncle is one of the biggest importers in Rome. We do all right. What about you? Do you live in the city centre?"

"Nah. I live on the way out to Salford. I just fancied a drink."

"That's my win then. I wasn't up for another night staring at the walls of my room. I'd much rather it be an attractive man."

Liam knew he would be blushing. Even at school, they had teased him for being able to go bright red at the drop of a hat. At twenty-six, he was most definitely a man, but he still felt like a boy in the eyes of Jonny, Harry and the rest of the gang.

They were at the bar and Marco opened the door, allowing Liam to walk in. Self-consciously, he walked past him, feeling totally unsettled at being so close to this handsome man. Thankfully, in the absence of a major game on that night, they had the bar to themselves. Liam gestured to an empty banquette in the corner.

"Pint?" he offered.

Marco nodded. "When in Rome…or not in Rome, I suppose."

The ease with which Marco talked had an infectious quality. Liam relaxed and went to the bar. He could do this, whatever it would be. For the millionth time, he wished he had the confidence of someone like Deano.

"Two pints of Strangeways, please," he said to the bartender.

As he waited, he caught sight of Marco in the enormous mirror that lined the bar. He sat with his arm around the back of the booth, taking it all in. He seemed so relaxed anyone would think he lived there instead of Liam.

They caught each other's eyes, and Marco winked, that cheeky smile creeping over his face again. Liam looked away, grateful that the barman had returned with the drinks.

Come on, Moseley. He's serving it on a bloody plate to you.

He paid and carried them over. He could feel Marco watching him and desperately tried not to spill on his shirt. It would be typical of him to make a total fool of himself before they'd even said more than hello to each other.

But mission accomplished, and once he'd settled himself in the curved booth, he raised his glass. "Cheers."

Marco followed suit. "To new friends. Pale and interesting."

They took a sip and Liam glanced over at him. He seemed to be totally oblivious to the effect he had on Liam. Maybe he wasn't blushing after all. Or maybe Marco had grown used to his gifts.

"So you're Manchester born and bred?" Marco asked.

"Can't you tell by the accent?" Liam replied.

Marco beamed. "I love the Manc accent. It's so…expressive."

"That's the first time I've heard it called that before," Liam said. "I'd rather have an Italian one."

"You find it sexy?"

Marco's eyes dared him to answer honestly. Something about this guy gave Liam confidence. No man had ever had this effect on him. "Yeah, I do," he replied before glancing down.

"Why do you do that?" Marco asked, leaning forward, his elbows on the table.

"Do what?" he asked.

"Break eye contact every time you say something. Are you ashamed?"

Liam shifted uncomfortably. "No, it's not that."

"Tell me what it is, then?" Marco asked, his voice soothing and sincere.

"I guess I don't think I have anything to say worth listening to," he replied, eventually.

To his astonishment, Marco's foot connected with his leg. The pressure told him it was absolutely on purpose.

"I respectfully disagree, Liam. I think I'd listen to you. Whatever you had to say."

He had that burning sensation on his neck again. It had made him so paranoid at school.

"Sorry, I have made you blush," Marco continued.

"Don't worry about it. I always bloody blush. They called me Po at school because of it."

Marco frowned. "What?"

"The red Teletubby?" Liam expected him to burst into that laughter again. Most people did when he confided this, but instead, Marco just shook his head.

"Kids can be so cruel. But who cares? They are in your past."

"Yeah, they're probably sweeping up shit in the hospital now. Serves them right."

This time Marco did seem amused. "Said with true passion. I like it. So, what do you do, Liam?"

Here it came. The inevitable question. He could hardly say he was a lackey for one of the biggest gangsters in the northwest of England, so he reverted to his stock answer. "Oh, you know, bit of this, bit of that. How about you?"

"As I said, my uncle works in shipping. I'm over here seeing if there is any potential to expand to Manchester."

Liam nodded. "The city is booming. You could do a lot worse."

"That's what I thought. I like what I see more and more."

The look which followed that statement practically oozed with intent. This time, Liam forced himself to meet Marco's gaze. "I've never been to Italy, but maybe I should," he replied. "Rome seems pretty good from where I'm sitting."

"Ah, you definitely should," Marco said, leaning back. "It is beautiful. I've been the length and breadth of it with my job. I worked in Venice recently. *Bellissima.*"

Liam had seen pictures of the water world on television. "Better than the canals in Manchester. They're just full of shopping trolleys and used condoms."

Marco laughed again. It was so loud and carefree that Liam had to stop himself from looking around to see if anyone noticed. But he forced himself to relax and ended up giggling along with him. It had been so long since he'd done something like this.

"This is better," Marco said.

"What is?"

"You are relaxing. You seemed very tense earlier," Marco said. "I thought perhaps you'd changed your mind about me."

"Oh, nothing like that," Liam said hurriedly. "It's just that I'm not out, you see. I don't normally do this."

Marco's stunning eyes widened. "Who isn't out these days?"

Shaking his head, Liam took a swig of his drink. "Me," he said, placing the drink down. "In my line of work, it isn't the done thing."

A group of lads banged through the door. Liam frantically scanned each face but didn't recognise any of them.

"Wow. I can't imagine being in the closet. At my eighteenth birthday party, I came out. I figured if I had to enter adulthood, people should know what they were dealing with. Although I like to make a statement now and then. It keeps them on their toes."

The lads were being quite rowdy. Even the barman appeared nervous.

"You're very brave," Liam said.

"Not really. My uncle is gay too, so it was a well-beaten path. No one in our family cares as long as you're healthy and happy."

"Sounds perfect."

Marco chuckled, but Liam couldn't relax. He watched the group of lads out of the corner of his eye. He could spot trouble a mile off, and these lads were desperate for it.

"We're a long way from perfect, believe me," Marco said. "But we get by."

Liam drained his glass. "You want another?"

Marco shook his head. "There are a lot of things I'd like from you, Liam…but another drink is not one of them."

The change in tempo took Liam by surprise. Heat crept over his face and he didn't know what to say in return. He had never been any good at the whole game-playing thing. "Just nipping to the loo," he managed before bolting for the door.

The gents' were downstairs, and thankfully he had it to himself. Staring at his reflection in the mirror, he tried to understand what Marco saw. Marco could walk down Canal Street in the Gay Village and have his pick of every muscle queen in town. Why had he chosen to spend his time with a skinny scally like Liam?

The door opened behind him and one of the lads from the group came in. He swaggered over to the sinks. *Why does everyone in Manchester think they're in Oasis?*

"You're one of Jonny Wellingham's lads, aren't you?"

Anxiety flooded Liam's system like the drugs they sold to a clamouring local market. He leant against the wall. "Yeah, what of it?"

"Got any gear for sale?"

Relief washed over him. At least this guy wasn't after trouble, but it made Liam remember that he had a face known in Manchester, whether he liked it or not.

"Sorry, mate. Off duty tonight. Give me fifteen and I'll have someone outside."

The lad winked at him and went over to the urinal. With a shaking hand, Liam typed a message to Deano that he had a customer waiting in the bar. "He's on his way."

"Cheers, lad."

Liam bolted out of the bathroom and up to a waiting Marco. "Come on, then," Liam said. "How about you show me one or two of the things you want from me?"

"That would be my pleasure," Marco replied. He looked Liam up and down, biting his lip. "Most definitely."

Marco set off out of the bar. Liam swallowed hard.

You can do this.

Trying not to look too fearful, he followed. His eyes were drawn to Marco's muscular legs and firm arse that were filling his jeans. What would they feel like?

Liam wished they'd had another drink for courage. He would look like a skinny beanpole next to this buff guy. But he would never see him again anyway. The next few hours would be all about pleasure and nothing more.

He followed Marco out onto the street...his heart thudding like a kettle drum.

Chapter Five

Marco pressed the key card against the lock and opened the door. As soon as they got into the room, Marco grabbed Liam by the waist and pulled him close, the pent-up chemistry from the bar finally allowed to bubble over.

Marco's lips were soft, yet his stubble scratched at Liam's face as they kissed. But the hunger with which his lips met Liam's almost overpowered him. He felt wanted and alive. Liam shuddered as Marco gently pushed his tongue into his mouth. On the walk over to the hotel, Liam had convinced himself just to go for it. Now, he couldn't wait to get naked with this gorgeous man.

His hands were shaking in anticipation as he undid Marco's shirt. They broke the kiss for Liam to pull it open to reveal a ripped body with just a smattering of hair covering his chest, forming a happy trail down his six-pack.

God, he was perfect.

In return, Marco dragged Liam's T-shirt over his head and threw it down on the floor. He ran his hands over Liam's slender body, twisting his nipple. The sensation of that first touch sent shivers through Liam's body. They kissed again, their bodies melding together, and that first feeling of Marco's body heat gave Liam tingles.

Liam dropped to his knees. Marco's cock strained against the material of his navy chinos. He stepped out of his expensive loafers and licked his lips, as if anticipating Liam's next move.

Liam reached up and took hold of Marco's brown leather belt, dragging it open. Steadying his fingers, he undid the button and unzipped the fly, the back of his knuckle grazing against the hardness underneath. His mouth watered at what might lie beneath.

Even that light touch made Marco moan. Liam pulled Marco's trousers down, so they fell to his ankles, revealing white CK briefs. They contrasted perfectly with Marco's olive skin. But Liam couldn't stop to enjoy the aesthetics. In a flash, he yanked the briefs down too.

Finally released, Marco's cock stood long, thick and proud. Unable to resist, Liam leant forward and took the tip in his mouth. Marco moaned and ran his hands over Liam's head, as Liam sucked hard at the tip, encasing it with his lips. The slight salty taste of pre-cum made his tastebuds come alive.

"Oh, God. More," Marco instructed.

Liam stared up, catching the need in Marco's eyes. It felt so powerful to have this stunning man asking for more. He let the cock fall out of his mouth and lightly licked Marco's balls, which hung low and contracted at his touch. Then, quick as a flash, he ran his tongue up the length of Marco before taking him in his mouth.

Marco stumbled backwards at the sudden sensation, gripping onto the chair nearby for support. *"Oh, cazzo si,"* he cried out.

Liam held him there for a second, then pulled back. Running his lips along the hard shaft almost to the end, he dove down again. His own cock pressed uncomfortably against the confines of his boxers.

Marco ran his hands through Liam's dark blond curls. "Fuck, you're amazing," he panted.

Reaching down, Marco helped him up. To Liam's surprise, Marco took hold of him and pushed him against the wall, face forward. Marco ran his hands around Liam's waist and licked up his spine. "You haven't seen anything yet," he murmured in Liam's ear.

His breath sent shockwaves of pleasure down Liam's spine. He didn't usually like being caught like this, but something about Marco told him he could trust him. He was hardly going to say no now, with his body crying out for more of what this man could give him.

Lightly tracing his fingers up and down Liam's torso, Marco found the button on his jeans. Kissing the back of Liam's neck, he unbuttoned them and dragged them to the floor. All his nerves were on fire and begging for this man's touch. Marco's hard cock, which had filled his mouth seconds earlier, pressed against his arse.

Marco plunged his hand inside Liam's boxers and gripped his dick, making Liam cry out. He had totally given the power to Marco, but at the same time, he trusted him. It was a heady mix and something Liam had never experienced before.

"Very nice," Marco whispered in his ear.

He squeezed harder and slowly massaged. Liam was so turned on he thought he would come right then. With his other hand, Marco tugged at Liam's boxer shorts, dragging them down his legs and exposing his arse.

Not releasing his grip on Liam's cock, he pushed his whole bodyweight against him, sliding his own dick between Liam's legs. The slight pressure on his hole made him desperate for more.

"You want this?" Marco whispered in his ear.

"Yes," Liam whimpered. He wanted everything from this man.

Placing another light kiss on the back of his neck, Marco let go of Liam's cock and rested his hands on Liam's waist. He gently flexed his own hips so his cock ran up and down the inside of Liam's thighs. The head of his cock, still damp from Liam's mouth, made contact with his balls.

Following the trail of his spine, Marco planted kisses all the way down as he sank to his knees. Liam wanted to do everything with this guy. He had a strange effect on him. Turning this way and that, Liam tried to see what Marco was doing but the hand on his waist stayed him. Marco's breath travelled down his body, making Liam slap sweaty palms onto the wall to steady himself. His heart thudded in his ears.

"You are incredible," Marco said. Letting go of Liam's waist, he ran his hands over his arse cheeks, forcing them apart.

"*Please*," Liam whined. All his sensations were focused on that one spot that was inches from Marco's mouth. He felt exposed and powerful all at the same time.

Marco blew lightly and the tickling sensation sent little explosions up Liam's spine. When Marco ran his tongue over him, Liam cried out and spread his legs as wide as the jeans and boxers still encasing his ankles would allow.

Marco licked up and down and each time he reached Liam's hole, he lapped at him with the flat of his tongue. The decisive strokes made Liam see stars. He had never felt such pleasure before and when Marco tried to reach around to take hold of his cock again, Liam had to bat his hand away. He didn't dare let him for fear it would all be over.

When Liam thought he could take no more, Marco stopped.

"Let's take this over there," he said, kissing Liam's arse cheek.

Liam didn't need telling twice. When Marco collapsed onto the bed, Liam stepped out of his trousers and boxers, throwing his socks onto the floor. Marco lay there, his arms open wide. Liam knew he wouldn't be able to last too long.

Straddling Marco's hips, he leant forward and kissed him. He could taste the beer from before on his tongue and the musky scent of Liam was still on him. Marco gripped the back of Liam's head with one hand and his arse with the other. In turn, Liam reached underneath him to massage Marco's magnificent cock. God, he wanted that inside him. His hole, still wet from Marco's tongue, cried out for it.

Then Marco flipped him over so Liam lay on his back, his legs wrapped around Marco's waist. Marco's solid muscle made Liam gasp as he felt his weight on him for the first time. His heels pressed against the firm flesh of Marco's arse. He had an incredible body, but his attentiveness didn't make Liam feel shy once.

Marco sat back on his heels and stared down at Liam. "You have no idea how sexy you look right now."

He ran his fingertips along Liam's torso. Liam arched in response, letting the sensation wash over him. Closing his eyes, he wanted to remember every moment.

Marco took hold of Liam's cock again and leant forward, engulfing it in his mouth. It made Liam cry out.

"I won't last…"

But Marco didn't seem concerned. He cradled Liam's balls as he sucked hard. Liam opened his eyes to see Marco's head bobbing up and down as he expertly sucked his cock. What this man could do with his mouth was insane. He knew the orgasm would take him past the point of no return and tried to move. But Marco rested him, placing a hand on his hipbone, gently forcing him to relax and let it happen.

Liam gripped the edge of the bed, bunching up the sheets as Marco ran his lips up and down his shaft. "I'm going to come. Oh, God. Marco."

His balls were desperate for release, and he came hard, his orgasm flooding through his body. Marco didn't stop sucking his cock. His body juddering, Liam could take no more. Taking the cue, Marco let his cock fall out of his mouth.

"You taste amazing," he murmured.

Liam's heart felt as though it would burst out of his chest. Panting, he let his head fall back on the pillow. But Marco wasn't finished with him. He straddled Liam's spent cock.

Reaching out and gripping Marco's cock with one hand, Liam ran his other hand over his smooth arse cheek. Marco slowly fucked Liam's palm, his arse sliding over Liam's dick. Marco closed his eyes, seemingly lost in the sensation as he twisted at his own nipples. Then he opened his eyes, batted Liam's hand away and took over working himself. Marco moaned and ran his arse over Liam's cock.

"Come for me," Liam murmured.

Marco pressed his free hand against the leather headboard, tugging at his cock hard with the other. "Oh, fuck yeah. You want it?" he grunted.

"Yes. Please."

Marco let out a cry and gripped Liam's waist so tightly with his thighs that Liam thought he might break. Then Marco threw his body back, his orgasm exploding out of him and falling onto Liam's body.

"*Si, si, si.*"

Falling forward, he kissed Liam hard. Their bodies sealed by his cum, they kissed for what seemed like an age. Liam gripping Marco's shoulders and Marco tenderly holding Liam's face.

Then they broke, and a sweaty Marco lay on his back. He turned and grinned at Liam. "Not bad for a start."

He got off the bed and returned from what must have been an en suite with a towel. Throwing it to Liam, he watched him clean himself up. "You are a sexy man, Liam... I don't know your surname."

"Moseley," Liam said. "And you?"

"Ponti."

"It sounds way more glamorous than bloody Moseley."

Marco got onto the bed next to Liam. He snaked his arm around his waist and drew Liam to him, so his head rested on his chest. "You need to stop putting yourself down, Liam Moseley. You are incredible."

No one had ever called him incredible before. Even though he suspected this stranger was probably just telling him what he wanted to hear, Liam liked it.

They lay together, the contentment like a drug. The traffic noise of Manchester played like a symphony outside, but it could have been a million miles away from the little world they had created in the hotel room.

"Will you stay with me tonight?" Marco asked.

"Are you sure? You don't have to. I know the drill," Liam replied.

"What is the drill?"

"Most people want me to go."

Liam couldn't remember the last time he had lain in someone's arms. Most businessmen were feeling guilty about wives or husbands at home before Liam had even retrieved his boxers from the floor.

"I don't want you to go," Marco said.

The emotion that those words inspired threatened to overwhelm Liam. Tenderness did not feature very highly in his life. It never had. His chest felt tight as he stared into Marco's earnest eyes. Every instinct told Liam to get out of there. To keep in control. Then the thought of waking up with those muscular arms around him took over.

"Then I'll stay," he managed.

Marco stroked his hair. As the summer evening turned to night, they dozed in each other's arms.

Suddenly, Liam's phone rang. Even worse, the ringtone that blared out meant one person only.

He leapt up. "Shit. I need to get that."

He raced over to his jeans and fumbled in the pocket. A bleary-eyed Marco watched him.

"Hello?" Liam answered the call.

"Where are you?" Jonny said gruffly.

"Just in town. What's up?" Liam replied.

"Meet us outside the cathedral. Twenty minutes."

The phone went dead. The real world wasn't as far away as it had seemed.

"I'm sorry," Liam said. "I've got to go."

Marco glanced at his watch. "It's just gone ten. What on earth is going on?"

"A friend in need," Liam offered.

The disappointment on Marco's face made Liam want to throw his phone away and never leave that room again.

"We were just getting going," Marco said.

"I'm sorry. Really, I am."

Marco got up off the bed and wrapped his arms around Liam. Their cocks pressing together threatened to make Liam very late for Jonny, but he knew that would be a terrible idea. Jonny had that tone that meant something big had kicked off.

Marco kissed him on the lips. He'd probably meant it as a goodbye kiss but once more the connection between them took on a life of its own. Marco pushed his tongue into Liam's mouth and Liam's cock sprang to life in response. God, he wanted this man again and again. He couldn't. Breaking apart, Liam wiped his mouth. "I can't. As much as I want to."

"Then you will have to give me your number, won't you?"

"You don't have to do that." Liam shook his head sadly.

"I don't do anything I don't want," Marco said, a steely determination in his eyes. "And I want all of you, Liam Moseley."

He felt torn. He had never given his number to a random hook-up before. He didn't want his different lives getting too close to each other. But he also desperately wanted to spend more time with Marco. He had an inner strength that Liam found totally irresistible. He wanted to lie in his arms and find out things about him. He wanted to see what he looked like first thing in the morning, sleepy and vulnerable. Most of all, he wanted to be fucked by him. After another second of indecision, he grinned. "Fair enough."

Squirming out of Marco's grip, he went over to the dressing table and wrote his number down on the pad there. "How long are you in Manchester for?" he asked as he retrieved his clothes.

Marco flopped down on the bed again, putting his arms behind his head and watching Liam. "No end date yet. I stay until the work is done."

Liam glanced at him. His muscles bulged all over. It was so difficult to leave such a perfect man, but Liam's fear of Jonny outweighed any amount of lust.

"My flat is ready this week. Maybe you could help me christen it?" Marco continued with a wink.

Liam had managed to get most of his clothes on and dashed into the en suite to rearrange his hair. He really didn't want the lads getting wind that he'd been doing anything other than having a few pints in town.

"I can definitely do that," Liam said, feeling bolder than he ever had before.

Satisfied with the reflection in the mirror, Liam went through to the bedroom. Marco still lay there and it was so hard to leave him. All Liam wanted to do was throw his clothes off and spend the night making Marco come and come. His two lives had clashed, but Liam knew better than to piss Jonny off for a man who would be a stranger again in no time.

Marco took hold of his hand. "Next time we switch your bloody phone off."

"I promise." Liam smiled. He had started to believe that Marco would actually ring him.

Marco lifted his chin up and Liam kissed him. Then he stood. "I really have to go."

"Until next time, then."

"Until next time."

At the door, Liam took one last look at Marco. He was wrapped in a sheet with his torso exposed, his hand flat on his stomach and the other behind his head.

God, I hope he rings.

Chapter Six

Liam walked through the backstreets across town. He could still smell Marco on his skin. That had been so fucking fantastic but cut way too short. There was so much more he wanted to do with Marco. He had to be realistic though. Everyone said they would call...and they never did.

He wanted to ring Claire to tell her. But it had gone ten — she would be hard at work, and she would go mad if he disturbed her. It would have to wait.

The streets were full of people staggering from one bar to another. Liam liked a drink and he wasn't one to shy away from other things, but he never understood getting absolutely obliterated. A childhood of sitting on the stairs with his brother watching their mum with her ever-changing line of boyfriends getting out of it on one substance or another meant he didn't like to lose control.

He turned onto Deansgate, the street that cut through the centre of Manchester. Bars were pumping out dance music and drinkers spilled out onto the pavement. These were his bread and butter. The citizens of Manchester were partying as hard as ever. Jonny relished this. He would stop at nothing to protect his position as the top dog of the city.

The cathedral lay slightly off the beaten track for nightlife. A couple of ancient pubs stood nearby, but they were pretty empty. Liam scanned around and saw Deano lurking in the grounds of the cathedral. He went over. "Why don't you try to look a bit more dodgy?"

Deano scowled. "Why don't you fuck off?"

"What are you doing, anyway?"

Deano sighed. "Waiting for you, dipshit. Come on."

They walked across the street and down a side street. Jonny and Harry were sitting in a van with the lights off.

"What's happening?" Liam said when he reached the driver's window that Jonny wound down.

"Davey King has been spotted. Little bastard has been on the missing list for a week. Give you one guess why."

Harry sighed. "You don't know that, Jon. Dave's been dealing this patch for ten bloody years. He's one of our best. Surely he deserves the benefit of the doubt."

Jonny slammed his hand down on the dashboard. "I'll give him the benefit of the fucking doubt. But I'll scare the living bastard daylights out of him just to be sure. That all right with you, Harry?"

Harry stayed silent.

"How do we do it, then?" Deano asked.

"He's in the Mitre," Jonny said. "He'll have his usual minders around him. We need a diversion, then lift him."

They had done things like this hundreds of times before, but Liam always got waves of anxiety washing through him. Sometimes he loved the buzz. After being in bed with Marco, he was full of adrenalin. It just needed channelling.

"Then back to yours, Jon?" he asked.

Jonny shook his head. "No, we'll go somewhere nice and quiet. He's as soft as shit on his own. He won't take much persuading. No need to upset Sadie and Pandora."

"What diversion we doing then?" Deano asked, his face a picture of excitement. He always wanted to be the leader of every job.

But this time Jonny turned to Liam. "You go inside. Keep your head down. I don't want them seeing you. Go straight to the loos. They never empty the bins in that place. Chuck a fag butt in one, get it burning."

"Burn the pub down?" Liam said, wide-eyed.

"No, you dozy twat. Just enough for them to evacuate everyone. When the fire brigade looks, someone had a crafty fag in the bogs. Fuck's sake, Liam. Once they're all out, Deano grabs Davey. We'll be waiting by the cathedral."

Deano frowned. "He's not going to come just like that, is he? Am I supposed to invite him to a bleeding party?"

Jonny leant across Harry and opened the glove compartment. He produced a nasty-looking knife with serrated edges that he handed to Deano. "Then you'll have to persuade him, won't you?"

"What about me, once I've set the fire?" Liam asked, half hoping that would be the end of it and he could dash back to Marco.

He would never be that lucky, though.

"You follow Deano. Make sure Davey doesn't get all brave and try to make a run for it. You can both ride with him. I've left everything in there for you."

Jonny winked at them.

Liam glanced at Deano, who gazed way too adoringly at the knife Jonny had given him. He hated working with Deano. He always had been a bloodthirsty little shit and had let that get the better of him on more than one occasion.

"Well? What the fuck are you waiting for? Closing time?" Jonny scoffed.

They didn't wait for Jonny to get more aggressive. Deano slipped the knife inside his jacket and they both set off to the pub.

"Try not to fuck this up." Deano sneered at Liam.

Liam ignored him. He focused on getting into the pub without any of Davey's goons seeing him. They all knew his face, of course. He'd dropped off product to them enough times.

But if Liam had a skill, it was going unnoticed. He had learnt that from an early age, when his mother's boyfriends would be glad of any excuse for trouble. It all lay in the body language. To his relief, the pub was busy. This wouldn't be a problem.

"You got cigs?" Deano asked.

"Yeah. You ready?"

Deano glanced over his shoulder. Jonny's beat-up old van had parked as close as possible without drawing attention. "Go for it."

Liam nodded. Ignoring the blood rushing through him, he stepped into the pub. With his head down, he crept through the crowd. The temptation to rush through had to be ignored—that would only bring attention to him. If he drifted slowly, no one would bat an eye.

He didn't look around. He could hear Davey holding court somewhere in the pub, his usual lackeys all listening intently. He sounded very pleased with himself.

At last, he made it to the gents. Inside, a couple of guys stood at the urinals, but mercifully, they weren't part of Davey's entourage. Liam stole into the cubicle and waited. One went, then the other.

Lighting a cigarette, he slipped into the main room. The bin by the sinks had been emptied. *What the fuck? When did they start cleaning this shithole?*

He wouldn't have long, so he dashed back into the cubicle and ripped the toilet roll holder off the wall. Three rolls were in there. He unravelled them and stuffed as much paper as he could into the bin.

Laughter and music were coming from the pub and twice he nearly abandoned the whole thing. The noises seemed to be coming clearer and his breathed a sigh of relief when he heard a woman shouting to her mates.

Once he'd filled about a third of the bin, he threw his cigarette into the paper. Just as he set off to leave, he saw a bottle of bleach left on the windowsill.

"Can't hurt to give it a bit of encouragement," he said to himself.

Liam squirted bleach around the edges of the bin. Even if forensics got involved, it would just seem like an over-eager cleaner hadn't rinsed the bin properly. Ten years with Jonny Wellingham had taught him how to be crafty.

Liam left the bathroom and hung around the rear of the bar. He had no need to make a hasty exit. They would all be doing that in a minute. It didn't take long. A drunk punter pushed past Liam to go into the toilet. Literally seconds later, he came dashing unsteadily into the pub, waving his hands.

"Fuck, the bogs are on fire," he shouted to no one in particular.

Just as the other customers started to take notice, the smoke alarm did its thing, and they were in the midst of a full-scale evacuation.

Betty, the landlady, took complete control. Lights went on, music stopped and she barked instructions at the top of her voice. The task of herding the drunk clientele out onto the street was no mean feat, but she seemed more than up to the job.

As she shoved people towards the doors, Liam managed to use a group of lads as cover to get out unnoticed. Outside pandemonium reigned supreme, but Davey's two bodyguards, Irfan and Alan, were stuck to him like glue.

"We need him on his own," Deano said, appearing at Liam's side.

Liam could see Irfan chewing frantically and scanning the crowd. Everyone knew he had a serious coke addiction, making him easy to provoke. Quick as a flash, Liam grabbed an empty pint pot from the table next to them and sent it sailing into the crowd. He aimed it perfectly, and it ricocheted off Irfan's bald head.

The heavyset man leapt into action. "Who the fuck threw that?"

Not waiting for a reply, he launched himself at the nearest man. But his target's group of mates weren't going to let that happen and it all kicked off. Alan and Irfan started throwing punches, which were met with the same from the group of lads. Davey, never one to get his hands dirty, scattered with the rest of the crowd.

Deano had already taken his cue and was by Davey's side in no time. Liam saw a quick exchange of words and Davey flinch at what must be the knife digging in his side.

Half dragging him to the van, Deano glanced back and Liam nodded, quickly following. The fight got into full swing just as a fire crew and police vans arrived.

Jonny and Harry were waiting in the van with the doors open. They hauled Davey inside, followed by Liam and Deano.

"What the fuck is going on? Liam, tell him. I meant to get in touch. Honest I did," Davey pleaded.

An iron frame had been crudely welded to the side of the van and two handcuffs were fixed on it. Deano and Liam fought with a struggling Davey to lock his wrists in place. As they managed to get him in place the van set off.

"For fuck's sake," Deano shouted through. "Give us a bastard chance."

Davey tried to wriggle out of their clutches. In the end, Deano slapped him across the face.

"Stop being a twat," he shouted in his ear.

They managed to get the handcuffs closed and fell backwards against the other side of the van, panting.

Davey's eyes flashed with terror. "Liam. Deano. Come on, lads. I've always been good to you. What's it all about?"

"You'll have to talk to Jonny about that." Deano said. "Now shut the fuck up."

He took way too much pleasure in these escapades. Liam couldn't say he didn't enjoy the rush, but he hated the violence. He saw it as a necessary evil, but Deano practically had drool on his lips.

They drove for the best part of an hour. Liam managed to tune out the sound of Davey begging for mercy. Even if Liam had the keys to the handcuffs, it would have been suicide to do anything against Jonny. After bumping around on an unsteady road for what seemed like an age, eventually the van screeched to a halt.

"You're fucked now." Deano sneered.

The doors opened and there stood Jonny and Harry. Jonny nodded to Liam and Deano. Obediently, they scrambled out of the van. Liam, glad to be as far away from Davey as possible, shuddered when he saw they were at Peak Quarry. Davey strained at the cuffs, but they were never going to give way.

"Davey, Davey, Davey. What am I going to do with you?" Jonny said, hopping in.

"What's this all about, Jon?" Davey said.

Jonny slapped him hard across the face. "We'll start with you not taking me for some mug. You know what this is about. Not heard from you in over a week, but a little bird tells me you've been dealing all over town."

A tear escaped Davey's eye and ran slowly down his face. Liam felt queasy. Davey might be a knob, but he was all right. He'd always been decent with Liam.

"I had a load of stock to get rid of, Jon," Davey babbled. "Honest I did."

Another slap.

"I said don't take me for a mug. Don't you think I track everything I give you and everything you sell, you dumb fuck? Harry loves a spreadsheet, don't you?"

"Love 'em," Harry said.

"All right. Listen, I can explain," Davey said, his nervous eyes glancing from Liam to Deano. "This guy. He approached me out of the blue. Said he's going to take Manchester. I thought I should do a bit of undercover, then tell you the score."

Jonny grabbed Davey's face, his fingers screwing Davey's mouth up. "Undercover work being to sell all the stock he could give you? How does that help me?"

Davey shook his face free. "He does everything remote, doesn't he? I never met him. He dropped the stuff off. I thought if I got his confidence, I might be able to find out more. Jonny, you have to believe me."

Leaning forward so his face was inches from Davey's, Jonny looked hard at him. "I don't have to believe anything. When is the next drop?"

"What?"

"The next drop. When and where?"

"Jon, I can't tell you that. He said if I did, he'd finish me."

Jonny shook his head and turned to Harry. "Crack on."

His eyes wide with fear, Davey watched Harry, who disappeared round the front of the van. "What's he doing?"

A cruel grin appeared on Jonny's face. "I've had this city sewn up for years, Davey. You know that. I can't have some little fuck come here and take over. I have to make an example of anyone who doesn't show me total loyalty, otherwise what will people think?"

"I've always been loyal to you, Jonny. Always. I've made you good money." Davey writhed, panic setting in now.

"The next drop," Jonny said.

"Jonny, please. He'll kill me."

Harry appeared with a petrol container. He jumped into the van and brushed past Jonny. Tearing off the cap, he poured the liquid around the inside of the van. Jonny hopped out.

"What makes you think *I* won't?" Jonny said, dusting his hands off.

Davey tried to kick out at Harry. "I'm begging you, Harry. Come on, mate."

Liam could barely watch, but he knew better than to look away. He'd done that once in the early days. That had earned him a beating from Jonny, who insisted his lads weren't squeamish.

Harry finished and jumped out of the van. The smell of petrol made Liam's eyes water.

"One last chance, Davey," Jonny said, taking out a lighter. "It's the night for fires tonight, isn't it? They follow you around."

"Fine. Drop-off is Tuesday. The bins behind the Printworks. He told me any time after ten-thirty. He just leaves the stuff in there and we pick it up. That's all I know, I swear."

"I believe you, Davey. I had every faith you'd remember which side your bread was buttered on."

"Course I do, Jon."

"Anything else?"

Davey shook his head. "Please, Jon. Don't burn me. Anything but that. I'm begging you."

Liam tensed. Davey should have just kept his mouth shut.

"We won't burn you. We're not that cruel," Jonny said. "Problem I have is, I don't fucking trust you. As soon as we drop you off in town, you'll be onto this new bastard telling him to change the drop-off. I'll be back to square one."

"I won't. I promise you."

Shaking his head, Jonny nodded to Deano and Harry. "I can't take that risk, Davey."

Harry and Deano pushed the van. Mercifully, Davey had no idea what lay in front of them.

"What are you doing? Come on, lads. The joke's over. I told you everything, I swear."

Resting his arm on Liam's shoulders, Jonny watched. As the van started to tip, Davey screamed his lungs out. Then gravity took over, and they heard Davey's wails cut through the air until an almighty splash sounded. Harry and Deano watched from the edge. Liam shuddered.

Deano had clearly never seen anything so hilarious in his life. But Liam felt sick. He had worked with Davey for years and always got on with him. They were all able to a man like Wellingham. Would he be tied up in a van one day?

Jonny turned to Liam. "Call us an Uber. There's a good lad."

Chapter Seven

A usual Manchester summer's day greeted him when he woke up. After the events of the previous night, Liam had barely had any sleep. Every time he closed his eyes, he could see Davey's fear. After a decade as a Wellingham Boy, things should have got easier, but they didn't.

Pushing the memories to the back of his mind, Liam grabbed his phone and saw that he had two missed calls and a message.

Couldn't stop thinking about you last night. Meet me at ten. At the doors to the Hilton hotel. We have unfinished business...

It was Marco. Liam could hardly believe he had heard from him and this soon. Throwing the duvet to one side, he leapt out of bed. The day after a kill, Jonny would usually chill out and give his lads the day off. Liam was determined to use it in the best way possible.

The rain pelted against the pavement as he dashed down the steps from the tram station. He walked through the underpass, stopping to put some coins in the homeless man's hat. When his brother Shaun had left Manchester, Liam had come close to being in that man's shoes. Thankfully, Harry had taken him in, and he never forgot that.

His heartrate sped up as he turned the corner. The next thing to greet him was Marco's beaming face. He stood outside the swanky Hilton hotel. How times had changed.

Seeing Marco grinning made the anxiety wash away.

"Well, hello," Marco said.

"Hiya," Liam said. "I didn't think I'd be seeing you this soon."

Marco playfully punched his shoulder. "My cock persuaded me to act sooner rather than later. I hope I didn't sound too desperate, but a deal is a deal."

Liam grinned. "You're right there."

"Come. Let me show you."

Marco pointed upwards. The hotel was housed in the Beetham Tower, Manchester's first skyscraper. Above that were very posh apartments. Liam had often stared up at the windows, picturing him and Claire living in one.

"Bloody hell, Marco. You've got one in there?"

Marco nodded. They walked around the building, away from the hotel doors. There a discreet reception with a concierge, which Liam hadn't even noticed before.

Remembering the feel of Marco's muscular body pressing him against the wall made excitement and nerves swamp Liam's system. "When this place was being built," he said, "we didn't know how bloody high it was going to go."

His mouth always ran away with itself when he was nervous. Marco simply replied with a smirk and licked his lips.

The lift came, and they got inside. Marco pressed forty. "Be careful, it makes your ears pop."

The lift set off and sure enough, Liam's ears popped like they had on the plane that time Jonny had taken the lads on holiday to Ibiza.

In close proximity to Marco, Liam had to pinch himself that he'd not only bedded him, but heard from him again.

"What are you thinking?" Marco asked.

"Nothing much."

"We're always thinking something. Tell me."

Liam sighed. "I didn't expect you to get in touch. That's all."

"You think I'm a liar?" Marco asked, frowning.

"No, not that…"

Liam's words were getting jumbled, and mercifully the lift bell rang, signalling they were here. But Marco's smile seemed to centre Liam. He couldn't be sure if Marco was being serious or playing with him. Liam quite liked that.

"Come on, let me show you."

Liam didn't know if Marco meant the flat or something else, but he walked down the corridor after him. It felt so plush and expensive. Photos of Manchester lined the walls, and it all smelt new. "This carpet is nicer than anywhere I've ever lived," he exclaimed.

"You been in a few places?" Marco asked.

Liam laughed bitterly. "My mum went from one man to the other. Let's just say, me and our Shaun had a few bedrooms."

They stopped and Marco slipped his key in the lock. Then he opened the door with a flourish, pointing for Liam to go in first.

A stunning apartment greeted him. Not huge, but it was absolutely gorgeous. A little corridor led down to a large living space with a lounge area on the left, complete with a gigantic television. On the right sat a kitchen and dining area that looked like it had every gadget going. Everything else paled in comparison when Liam took in the view.

Through the floor-to-ceiling windows, the whole of Manchester lay before him. The streets he had grown up in were crisscrossed and looked totally different. Far below, people were dashing up and down, going about their business.

"Fucking hell," Liam said, running over to the windows and pressing his nose against the glass.

Marco dumped his keys down on the dining table and walked up behind him. Feeling him there made Liam think about the night before in the hotel. He leant against his body and shuddered as Marco wrapped his arms around his waist.

"Not a bad view, eh?" Marco murmured.

"I'll say. I bet it looks ace at night."

"Why don't you stay and find out?"

Liam spun around to face Marco. "I'd love it."

Marco kissed him. A deep, hungry kiss that Liam matched. Liam's cock instantly hardened. This guy had a powerful effect on him.

They broke the kiss, and Marco smiled. "I'm glad you didn't make me wait too long."

"Is there a bedroom in this place?" Liam replied.

Marco led him by the hand through the living area to a bedroom at the rear. The white décor made quite the statement — carpet, walls and bedding.

"It's like being in a cloud," Liam exclaimed. "How come you got everything set up so quickly?"

Marco sat on the end of the bed. "I threw money at it, of course."

He pulled Liam towards him. Liam gasped as Marco reached underneath his T-shirt and across his stomach. Gently, he leant down and kissed the exposed skin, tracing his tongue around Liam's belly button.

He took such care and Liam trembled with anticipation of the day that lay ahead of him. It wasn't even lunchtime. People all around were getting on with their working day and he lay high above them without a care in the world. This time, no one would spoil their fun.

Marco took Liam's T-shirt off and let it drop to the floor. He ran his hands up Liam's taut body and down his arms, ending by holding his hands. He planted kisses along the waistband of Liam's jeans, making him judder.

Stopping, Marco stared up with a cheeky glint in his eye. "He's ticklish."

Liam stuck out his tongue. Still maintaining eye contact with Marco, he undid the buttons on his jeans. He took Marco's hand and pressed it against his groin.

"He's hard too," Marco teased.

"Is there any wonder?" Liam replied.

"Show me."

Liam kicked off his trainers. He enjoyed the hunger in Marco's eyes. Slowly, he took his jeans down, stepping out of them and his socks so only his boxers remained. Before he had set off, he had agonised over what to wear. Little did he know the carefully planned outfit would be in a ball on the floor in minutes.

His black boxers did nothing to hide his arousal, and he palmed his cock. Marco watched him, making him feel all the hornier. Marco enjoyed the tease. He'd made that clear the other night. This time, Liam would play.

"You are so gorgeous," Marco murmured.

"You like?" Liam asked.

Marco nodded.

"Show me," Liam added.

He had no idea where this confidence had come from, but he liked it. So did Marco, judging by the ever-present grin. Marco stood up. Shrugging his hoodie off, he threw it on the floor. Underneath he had a tight white vest which showed off his muscles to perfection.

He soon threw it in the corner. Next came his shorts. He let them fall to the floor and kicked them away. Once again, he had on tight white briefs. Even though Liam had already sampled what was underneath, he couldn't fight the anticipation that turned his legs to jelly.

"Now who goes first?" Marco said.

Liam reached forward and pulled him close by the waistband of his briefs. They locked lips and Liam grabbed hold of Marco's tight arse with both hands. Their hard cocks rubbed together, separated only by flimsy cotton. Perhaps the anticipation thing was overrated. Liam could wait no more. He intensified the kiss, grabbing the back of Marco's head with one hand and delving the other under the cotton to feel the soft, toned skin that lay underneath.

Marco returned the favour by slipping his hand under the waistband of Liam's boxers and encircling his cock with his fingers. Liam let out a sigh as the waves of sensation flooded through him.

They broke the kiss, and Liam dragged his boxers off. "You win," he declared, falling on the bed.

Marco followed suit and, once naked, crawled onto the bed next to him. "Then I claim my prize," he said, wrapping his arms around Liam.

They kissed again, and the feel of their fully naked bodies melding together couldn't have been more perfect. The super-king bed could have been their own private island, and they rolled from one side to the other in a mass of entangled limbs, Marco's cock grinding against Liam's. He let out a moan. Their coming together was even more intense this time around, if that were possible.

Marco's luxurious citrussy scent swamped Liam's senses, firing him. He wanted to explore every inch of Marco. The initial nerves evaporated and Liam took control. With Marco on his back, Liam took his thick cock in his hand. He leant down and wrapped his lips around the head, staring up at Marco as he did.

Marco closed his eyes and sighed, his body visibly relaxing at Liam's touch. Agonisingly slowly, Liam moved down his dick until he had the whole of him in his mouth. He held it there for a second, the thick head sitting perfectly in the roof of his mouth. Liam sucked, making Marco tense. He loved giving him pleasure. Quickly he slid his mouth up and down Marco's shaft, the change in tempo making Marco cry out.

But he didn't want it to end there this time. Liam stopped and crawled up Marco's body. He locked lips with him again and they kissed. "Fuck me," he whispered.

He needed this so badly that he hadn't been able to focus all morning. Marco leapt into action. He rolled Liam onto his back and gripped his ankles, moving them up, and Liam twitched at the first touch of Marco's tongue to his exposed hole that cried out for attention.

He grabbed his own thighs. Marco responded by running his nails down Liam's legs, and the touch jolted like electricity.

Marco licked and teased him. He deftly alternated between his tongue and his finger, getting Liam's hole ready for him. Every touch made Liam moan. He didn't want to wait any longer. He needed to be fucked — hard. "Please, Marco."

Marco reached across to a washbag on the nightstand and found a condom and packet of lube. Never breaking eye contact with Liam, he opened the packet and squeezed a generous portion onto his finger. Gently rubbing it against Liam's hole, he pushed his finger deep inside. The burn made Liam pull his legs farther apart, giving Marco all the access he needed. His body shuddered as Marco slid two fingers inside, stretching and prepping. "God, you feel good," he murmured.

The waiting drove Liam crazy. He tried to reach for Marco's cock, but Marco held him in place with his other hand. He had no doubt who held the control, and Liam liked it.

After what seemed like an age, Marco ripped the condom wrapper open with his mouth and pulled out the condom. He deftly rolled it onto his cock with his free hand while still letting his fingers open up Liam as much as possible. He slathered the rest of the lube on and, removing his fingers, pressed the head of his cock against Liam's arse.

Liam needed this so badly he was nearly begging. Marco pushed against the resistance and Liam cried out as the head of Marco's cock broke through. Marco slid slowly inside him, and Liam struggled to catch his breath, overwhelming passion burning through his body.

"Is that okay?" Marco asked.

The gentleness with which he entered Liam's body was lovely, but Liam had a fire that needed to be dealt with.

"Don't worry about me," Liam gasped. "Fuck me."

Once fully inside, Marco didn't wait for him to get used to it. Instead, he pulled out almost to the tip before pushing straight in again.

Again and again, Marco repeated the movement, each time getting faster. This was what Liam craved. His cock was solid and flat against his stomach. Marco had gained confidence now. This was the moment at the top of the roller coaster and Liam loved it.

"Oh, yeah." Liam groaned. "Harder."

Holding Liam's feet in place, Marco bucked his hips. Fucking him hard. Liam's panting matching his strokes. Marco found a pace and, making the bed shake, he was finally sharing Liam's urgency. His handsome face was full of fire and intent. Just when Liam thought he could take no more, Marco stopped and pulled out.

"What are you doing?" Liam panted.

"Turn over," Marco instructed.

Liam extracted his legs from Marco's grip and spun over onto all fours. Without missing a beat, Marco entered him again. Liam buried his face in the pillow to mask his cries. Marco gave him what he had pleaded for, slapping his arse cheeks as he did so.

"Oh God, Liam. You are so hot."

Their bodies slick with sweat, Marco held on to his shoulder as he pounded him. Liam reached underneath himself and stroked his own cock. He wanted to come so badly, but he also didn't want this to end.

"Liam, I'm going to come."

Liam pulled at his cock more furiously and when Marco dug his nails into his hips, he surrendered. His orgasm hit him like a truck. He dropped his face into the pillow and let out a yell. Pleasure radiated through his body, tensing his muscles and making him a slave to the pure sensation.

Marco fell onto his back, pressing Liam down onto the bed with him. They both lay there panting as Liam slowly came back to earth.

"You drive me crazy," Marco whispered in Liam's ear.

Liam couldn't even reply. He had never had such intense sex in his life. Marco walked over to the en suite. After flushing the toilet, he came back out with a towel that he threw to Liam.

"It was every bit as perfect as I spent most of last night thinking about," Marco said.

"Glad you didn't tell me that before," Liam said, cleaning himself up. "No pressure or anything."

"I hope your phone is on silent," Marco teased as he crawled onto the bed and wrapped his arms around Liam. He took the towel from his hand and threw it on the floor.

"This time, I'm going nowhere," Liam replied. "But wait, I got you a housewarming present."

Marco frowned as Liam wriggled out of his hold and hung over the bed, grabbing his jeans. Marco lazily stroked his arse cheeks as he did. Even though they were both spent, just the touch of him made Liam's body alive.

He produced a tin from his jeans pocket and snuggled back in the bed. Marco sat up on the pillow so they were side by side. Liam handed him the tin and Marco opened it to find a bag of Jonny Wellingham's finest weed.

"Now that is the kind of afternoon I can get on board with," Marco said with a smile.

Chapter Eight

The afternoon merged into evening, and Liam never wanted the spell to be broken. Jonny might be one of the biggest bastards in the northwest of England, but he provided good product. They had stayed in bed all day, alternating between smoking and fucking.

He should be exhausted, but he couldn't get enough. He had never been so content in all his life.

They were lying in each other's arms, Liam's head on Marco's chest. Kendrick Lamar played on the inbuilt speakers, and everything felt perfect...until Liam's stomach gave an almighty growl.

It was like a call to arms. Marco sat up, gently dislodging Liam from his chest. "You are hungry. What an awful host I am. My grandmother would cut my balls off."

Liam giggled. "It's fine, honestly."

But Marco would not be placated. He got out of the bed and put on a pair of jogging trousers from his open bag in the corner of the room. Throwing a pair of pyjama bottoms to Liam, he grinned.

"Come. I'll cook. I got some shopping this morning. Your supermarkets are full of crap, by the way."

Reluctant to leave the bed, Liam put the pyjamas on and followed Marco through to the kitchen area. Marco fiddled with his phone and put on some Dua Lipa, instantly livening the mood. He gestured to the dining table and forced Liam into a chair.

"You want wine?" he asked over his shoulder as he started to busy himself.

Usually a beer man, Liam didn't want to come across as unsophisticated and simply nodded. Marco took a bottle of white out of the fridge and poured them two glasses.

"Are you going to tell me where you had to rush off to last night?" Marco said, placing one of the glasses in front of Liam.

Liam wasn't sure if he liked this change in tempo. The grass had been strong, and he had been quite content to stay in their sex haze. But the real world had a habit of forcing its way into things, so he would have to go with it.

To buy himself some time, he took a sip of the drink. It tasted incredible, so many flavours exploding on his tongue. A far cry from the cheap sparkling muck that his mother used to go through by the bottle.

"A friend in need. Nothing major."

"You must be a good friend," Marco said, chopping vegetables he'd retrieved from the fridge.

"I guess so. Anyway, you haven't told me much about you," Liam countered. He needed to change the conversation. Today he wanted to leave the lies behind him.

"What is there to tell?" Marco said. "I grew up in Roma. My dad went away when I was very small, and my mother and my grandmother raised me. I'm a terrible spoilt brat."

"Only child?" Liam ventured.

"The worst kind," Marco said with a wink. "I always get what I want."

"Nothing wrong in that," Liam said, taking another swig of his wine. He admired people who went after their desires.

"I guess not. At eighteen, I went to work for my Uncle Zee. I've been with him ever since."

"That must have been a long time then," Liam said with a wink.

Marco stopped and threw a half-cut mushroom at him. It ricocheted off his head. "Cheeky bastard." Marco giggled. "I'm only thirty."

"Calm down, old man," Liam teased. He sat back in his chair and revelled in the wide grin on Marco's face. He loved the fact that he had put it there.

"How old are you? Thirty?"

Liam reached under his chair and retrieved the half mushroom, which he sent sailing back at Marco. "Twenty-six. What does your uncle do?"

He didn't know if he had imagined it, but a guarded look appeared on Marco's face. "I told you, we import things."

"What like?"

"Oh, this and that. Fashion mainly. I'm over here to see if there are any distributers that would be interesting. We need to diversify."

Liam got up and walked into the kitchen, placing a kiss on Marco's shoulder. A frying pan heated up on the hob and when Marco dropped chopped onion, ginger and garlic into it, the smell instantly made Liam realise he needed to eat. "How come you're diversifying?"

Marco shifted uncomfortably. "Let's just say I fucked up royally. We lost a lot and my uncle told me I either make this a success or I'm out. Simple as that."

He seemed so pained that Liam had to wrap his arms around him. He planted a kiss on his cheek. "Well, your uncle's loss worked out pretty good for me."

Instantly, the troubles on Marco's face disappeared. "And for me. Now scoot or I'll get distracted."

Liam resumed his seat at the table, albeit reluctantly.

"What about you?" Marco said, resuming his culinary theatrics. "Do you have family?"

"I have a brother, Shaun. He's four years older. You see, when I was still at school, my mum disappeared. No trace of her. The police said she'd gone abroad."

Marco stopped, his face a picture of concern. "Are you serious?"

Liam nodded. He rarely spoke about what became the worst thing to happen to him, and here he sat, talking about it over a glass of wine with a stranger. "Anyway, Shaun cared for me for a bit, but he wanted to get out of Manchester. So as soon as I hit eighteen, he went on his travels."

"Didn't you want to go with him?"

Liam thought back to that fateful day when Shaun had announced his plans. It had been two weeks after Liam's eighteenth birthday. Of course he'd asked Liam to go with him, but already the excitement of Jonny Wellingham had taken a hold of Liam. He had no desire to leave a city that had opened up to him.

"Nah. Not for me. Besides, my mum will come back one day. Imagine if she appeared and we weren't here."

He caught Marco looking at him with a mixture of interest and pity. The same look everyone gave him when he said something like that. But it felt worse on Marco's face somehow.

"The big bloody traveller only went and ended up in Blackpool anyway." Liam sniggered. He wanted to lift the mood. "He runs a B&B there for an ex-boyfriend of his."

"Two gay men in the same family?" Marco said, throwing mushrooms, peppers and a can of tomatoes into the pan. Another one had boiling water bubbling away, into which he tipped a generous portion of pasta.

"Yeah. Must be in the genes," Liam continued.

"Same in our family. My uncle is one of us and my cousin Enzo. My grandmother loves it."

"Your family all know?" Liam asked.

"I told you, I announced it as soon as I was eighteen."

"Shaun is the only person who knows about me. We told each other on the same night, not long after Mum had left. Oh, and my friend, Claire. But she's brilliant. Everyone else wouldn't understand."

The aroma filling the flat made Liam almost dribble. He couldn't wait to dig in.

Marco drained the pasta with a flourish, a big cloud of steam engulfing him. "If your friends don't understand, they aren't friends." He tipped the pasta onto two plates and covered it in the sauce from the pan. "Ta-da." He placed the meal in front of Liam and took a seat opposite him. "Just like Nonna used to make. Well, not quite. The ingredients in this town are not exactly up to Italian standards."

Liam gently kicked him. "Hey. Less of it. I'll have to show you some English cuisine."

"Fish and chips or overcooked meat? No thanks," Marco replied with a wink.

Liam wasn't much of a cook, but he had a list of the best takeaways in Manchester. That would have to do, although when he took the first forkful of pasta, he knew he had lost this argument. The tomato, garlic and pepper combo was perfection, and he couldn't get it in his mouth quick enough.

"You are hungry," Marco said.

"We worked up an appetite."

"That is true. You carry on refuelling. I need you at full strength. I'm not done with you yet."

Liam's phone, which he had left on the coffee table, vibrated. He reached across and picked it up.

"Phones at the dinner table?" Marco said. "Tut tut."

"Sorry. I'd better check it, though. Might be work."

He opened up the screen, and there was a message from Harry.

Tomorrow. The Arndale. Ten.

"Anything important?" Marco asked.

Liam locked the screen and slung the phone onto the chair behind him. "Nothing much. I've got to meet some workmates tomorrow at ten."

He hated his real life threatening the bubble they had spent all day creating. Marco stared at him. "What?" Liam asked.

"I wish we could stay here forever," he said sadly.

Liam reached across and took Marco's hand. "Me too. I never do this. I can't remember the last time I had sex with someone twice. That sounds awful when I say it out loud, doesn't it?"

Marco squeezed his hand. "No, just honest. I like that. I like you, Liam Moseley."

He blushed. Compliments were a rare thing in his world, and he found himself being more open with Marco than anyone else in his life, except for maybe Claire. "I like you too. I hope we get to see each other again."

"Oh, we will do. I will insist."

Liam flung his fork down onto his plate and launched himself at Marco. They kissed hard. Once again, the passion ignited like a bomb. Want and need ran through his system at a rate that took his breath away. It was intoxicating and terrifying at the same time.

What is this guy doing to me?

Marco's fork clattered to the floor as they staggered over to the couch and fell onto it, still kissing. Marco pulled Liam's pyjama bottoms from him. Liam lay back as Marco nestled between his legs, taking his cock in his mouth. Already semi-hard, his dick burst into life. Marco reached into his own jogging trousers to massage his cock.

Liam ran his hands through Marco's chocolatey-brown hair, soft without all the gel in it. It made him look younger and less intimidating. Marco sucked him and Liam writhed as the shivers overtook his body once more. He had come so many times that day, but it didn't make any difference. Nothing satiated him where Marco was concerned.

Marco's head bobbed up and down. Liam knew he wouldn't take long. He let out a moan and tensed.

"Oh no you don't," Marco ordered. "Bedroom now."

Obediently, Liam walked through. Marco had lost his jogging trousers and his hard cock stood proudly. Liam reached forward and massaged it. This time Marco groaned.

"God, that is incredible," Marco murmured.

With his other hand, Liam ran one of Marco's balls between his fingers. He squeezed ever so slightly, and Marco gripped his shoulder. He drew Liam closer, and they kissed.

Marco pushed Liam so he fell onto the bed, and crawled up his body. They kissed frantically again. Liam ran his hands through Marco's soft curls as Marco ground his cock against Liam's.

"Make me come, Marco. Please," he begged in Marco's ear.

Marco crouched between Liam's legs. "Make yourself come," he said. "For me."

Liam licked the palm of his hand and took hold of his own cock. Never losing eye contact with Marco, he began to run the palm of his hand over his cock. His balls ached when Marco did the same. Even with barely any skin contact, Liam was more turned on than he had ever been in his whole life.

He gripped Marco's waist with his knees. He was going to come. With his other hand, he ran his nails down Marco's thigh.

"Oh…"

Throwing his head back, he waited for the blissful moment of white. The orgasm ripped through him, sending him soaring. He cried out as he came over his taut belly. Marco got up on his knees and grunted, his cum falling onto Liam in hot spurts. It made Liam judder all over again.

Once again, holding on to the headboard with one hand, Marco leant down and kissed Liam. Then he reached for the towel on the floor and gently cleaned his body.

"No one has ever treated me like this," Liam said. The words had fallen out of his mouth without him thinking. The last thing he wanted to do was to scare Marco off by being needy, but something had begun to change within him.

Marco gave him that sad frown again. "That is a crime. You deserve so much more than you settle for, Liam."

Throwing the towel on the floor, Marco curled up against Liam and wrapped his arm around him. Liam was in very real danger of crying at this point. He put it down to post-sex hormones.

"We will not move from here until the morning," Marco announced.

"That sounds nice," Liam replied, stroking Marco's muscular, hairy forearm. "I'm sorry. I have to leave in the morning."

"Ah, I have a work thing to do tomorrow anyway," Marco said. "But I hope we can see each other again."

"I do too," Liam said lazily.

That night, for the first time since he and Shaun had shared a bed as kids, Liam settled down for sleep with the heat of another body next to him. Marco wrapped his arm around him and snuggled into his back. Liam revelled at feeling his warm breath between his shoulder blades.

Liam thought about how different his life could be if he ever found someone to do this with permanently. That would be the dream, but his life was not compatible. Even so, the visions of him and Marco doing couple things kept flashing into his mind.

Tomorrow, he would have to detach himself from this or people could get hurt. But for now, he entwined his fingers with Marco's and drifted off to sleep.

Chapter Nine

The Arndale Shopping Centre in the middle of Manchester had hardly anyone in it. It was a Wednesday and except for a few hardcore shoppers, most people would be at their desks earning the money to spend here at the weekends.

Liam sat in the overpriced coffee shop, sipping a tea. His body ached everywhere, and each time, it reminded him of the best twenty-four hours of his life.

Leaving Marco that morning had been almost impossible. Twice they had tried to get out of bed, but Marco's wandering hands and Liam's responsive cock made them stay under the duvet just a little longer. Marco had a remarkably high sex drive and Liam thanked his lucky stars, because he couldn't get enough of him either.

Is this what love feels like, or is it just lust?

Getting out his phone, he called Claire.

"What the fuck do you want?"

"That's a nice way to say hello to your best friend in the world," he replied.

"It's ten o'clock. I only got to bed three hours ago. It was bloody dead last night. I had one punter."

Liam frowned. They usually did a roaring trade six days a week—the punters tended to stay with their wives on a Sunday.

"How come?"

"Told you. This new guy is undercutting, and listen to this, Gina and Deb didn't show last night. I had to tell Jonny, and he went spare."

Liam could just imagine how that conversation had gone. It felt like whenever he had time for himself these days, things took a turn for the worse. "Have you spoken to them?"

"I messaged them. They've gone over to this fella. They're done with Wellingham. I really think I'm going to do it," Claire continued.

"Just you stay put," Liam urged. "This new guy won't be a problem after today."

"Shit. Is he making a move?" Claire asked. "Jonny will kick the living shit out of Gina and Deb if they try to come crawling back. I'll ring them later. We can come up with an excuse. Fuck, I'll put them in the hospital if I have to. Where are you?"

"The Arndale. We're doing a grab in a bit."

Claire whistled. "Poor bastard. Is that why you rang me?"

A smile crept over Liam's face. "That and..."

"You've met someone."

How the fuck does she do it?

"Yeah. Met him after you made me feel like an old maid the other night."

He could hear Claire sitting up in bed and lighting a cigarette. Now he had her attention. A mother sat nearby with a pram. He could just imagine her horror at listening in on the conversation that Claire would have in mind.

"Why didn't you tell me yesterday, you little shit?" she said, exhaling loudly.

"I met him again yesterday and spent the day and night at his."

"Fucking hell, that's a record for you, isn't it? Oh, Liam. How do you feel?"

An interesting question he hadn't dared ask himself. He had no idea what his feelings were except when he thought about Marco, a calmness fell over him. "I like him, Claire. He's Italian and gorgeous. Way out of my league."

"Hey, you, that's my best friend you're slagging off. Is he a good lay?"

"The best. But it's more than that. I don't know. He makes me laugh and..."

"And what? Don't tell me you're in love with him already. *Jesus*, Liam."

"No, of course not. But I reckon I would be if I let myself."

Claire exhaled. "You'd have thought I would have noticed hell freezing over."

"Fuck off." Liam chuckled.

The woman at the next step raised an eyebrow. Liam mouthed "*Sorry*." She shook her head.

"Seriously though, babe," Claire continued. "I'm really pleased for you. It's about time you realised there is more to life than being Jonny Wellingham's slave. Hang on, you said he was Italian?"

"Yeah."

"Is he just passing through, then?"

"Not sure. He works for his uncle and is setting up an office in Manchester. He'll be here for a bit."

Claire giggled. "Enough time for you to make him fall madly in love with you and whisk you away to Italy. Don't forget me when you're living it up in Rome or somewhere."

She had got a little ahead of herself. The idea of thinking about things past the next day made Liam anxious. At some point, he would have to level with Marco about how he earned his money and that would be that.

"Nah. I just want to enjoy it for what it is."

"Good for you. Are you seeing him again?"

He and Marco had agreed to meet the next day. The temptation to see him that night was great, but Liam had no idea what Jonny had in mind for this new dealer. Knowing his boss, it would be a drawn-out thing.

"Tomorrow night. I need a bit of recovery time."

"Ring sting? Vitamin E oil, love. Take it from a pro." She cackled. "Liam's love tunnel will be fresh as a daisy in no time."

"Claire!"

Jonny, Harry, Aleck and Jack walked into the food court. Liam waved them over. "They're here. I'd better go." Without waiting for her reply, he terminated the call.

"You look like shit," Harry said as they reached his table.

"Thanks," Liam replied. "Didn't sleep well."

Jonny narrowed his eyes. "You better not be on anything."

Typical Jonny. He only liked his lads to smoke a bit of weed. If he caught them taking anything else, they would be punished. He didn't like the idea of paranoia in his gang.

"I just couldn't sleep," Liam said sulkily.

Jonny swatted him over the head. "Calm down, Miss Cranky. Don't take it out on us because you were tossing all night."

Aleck and Jack sniggered.

"Where's Deano?" Liam asked.

Harry sat down at the Formica table next to Liam and took his tea from his hand. He took a swig. "He's got us a new van. We'll be needing it today."

"What's the plan?" Liam asked, grabbing his drink back from Harry.

Jonny sat on the other side of him. "Get us some brews, Jack."

Obediently, Jack went off.

"You go and see if he's there," Jonny said to Aleck. "Give me a shout when he is. If he moves before we get to you, follow him. We're taking this nice and easy. Got it?"

Aleck nodded and set off out of the shopping centre. Liam looked from Jonny to Harry and back again.

"This foreign twat is doing a drop-off for Davey at the back of the Printworks in a bit. It's the usual script. Sack on his head and into the van before he knows what's happening."

They had done this so many times.

"Then where?"

"My place," Jonny replied.

Jonny didn't usually like to bring violence home. He must be really rattled by this new guy.

"How come?" Liam asked.

"Something tells me this bastard will be tough to crack," Jonny said. He looked eerily determined. "Sadie's at her mum's, and I've bunged a load of notes to Pandora. She won't be home until she's spent it all."

"We get him in the pool house," Harry continued. "That's why we're bagging his head. Don't want him to know where the fuck he is."

It was a decent plan. Jonny had big gates to his house and the pool house lay far enough away for any noise to be easily disguised.

"I want to know fucking everything," Jonny sneered. "He must be working for someone. He has moved too bloody quickly for it to be one man. Someone is out to get me, and this piece of shit is going to give it up. Harry will make sure of that, won't you?"

Harry nodded grimly.

Many second-rate criminals had tried to hold out on Harry, but he had a seemingly endless supply of ideas to get information out of them. Liam shuddered. He almost felt sorry for the men who'd lost teeth, nails, fingers and once, balls. They all sang like canaries in the end.

He didn't fancy this new guy's chances. Jonny was more enraged than Liam had seen him in a long time. Jonny often let his temper loose, but seeing him controlled, almost clinical, chilled Liam. He hoped he would never be on the receiving end of a Jonny Wellingham intent on revenge.

Jack returned with the drinks and sat.

"Did I say you could sit down?" Jonny said.

Instantly standing up, Jack reddened. "Sorry, boss."

Jonny moved the chair with his foot. "Take a seat, Jack."

Embarrassed, Jack sat and tried to ignore the sniggers from Harry and Liam. Jack had only been in the gang about a year and still seemed to act like he was in a Guy Ritchie movie. Liam had seen his type come and go. He could tell on sight that he wasn't going to last, but Jonny would do his best to break him in.

"What time is the drop?" Liam asked.

Harry glanced at his watch. "Twenty minutes."

Jonny swigged from his coffee and leered at two young women who walked past.

"When did any of you lot get laid?"

Liam squirmed. He hated it when Jonny tried to be all chummy with them. It made his skin crawl.

"Last week," Jack said proudly.

"Porn doesn't count," Harry countered.

Laim's anxiety levels soared as Jonny's gaze fell on him.

"We all know Harry here is a monk. What about you, soft lad?"

Just as all three pairs of eyes practically burnt holes into Liam, Jonny's phone went off. Liam thought he might kiss whoever was on the line.

"Fuck, it's Deano."

On second thoughts...

"What is it?" Jonny barked into the phone. His face grew grave as he listened, and he shut the call off without saying a word. "Cute bastard is here already."

They all leapt up.

"Is Deano in place?" Harry asked.

"Just," Jonny replied.

They hurried through the shopping centre.

"Keep it calm, lads," Jonny said. "Don't draw attention."

They cut through to the exit, which led out onto the side street where Davey had been due to pick up the drugs. The entertainment complex known as the Printworks was housed in old newspaper offices. This dealer had chosen a clever location for during the week—there'd be enough people walking around to provide cover but not enough to clock what was going on. This guy knew Manchester well enough to choose this place.

The adrenalin kicked in when he saw the bins that the cinema used. It must be those.

He glanced farther and saw Deano sitting in a bright blue van. Aleck stood on the corner, waiting for them.

"Where is he?" Jonny said.

"In the van, of course," a smug Aleck replied.

Jonny stormed up to the van and yanked the door open. Deano sat in the driver's seat, clearly very pleased with himself. "All right, boss?"

The smug smile on his face vanished as Jonny dragged him from his seat and pushed him up against the van.

"Who the fuck told you to do that?" Jonny sneered.

"No one, boss," Deano stammered. "I just didn't want to lose him. I thought you'd be pleased."

"That's why I sent fucking Aleck. To follow him. What if he'd got wind of you two clumsy twats and done a runner? Don't you ever disobey me again." He let go of Deano and muttering to himself, made his way around to the back of the van.

"You stupid twat," Harry said. "You think you're on some fast track in this operation, don't you? It doesn't work like that."

Deano had the sense to stay quiet, and Harry went to join Jonny.

"Fuck off, Moseley," Deano managed, noticing Liam smirking at his fuck up.

Liam didn't even grace it with a reply.

When Liam got to the rear of the van, Jonny had the doors open and they saw a figure crouched in the back.

Deano had tied him up and put a bag on his head. He looked smaller than Liam had imagined.

"They did a good job, but I'll have both your bollocks if you tell them I said that," Jonny said. "Harry, you ride with Deano to mine. Just in case he has any other bright ideas. Liam, you, me and the others in my car. Come on."

Liam, Jack and Aleck followed Jonny to the multistorey where his Mercedes SUV waited. Jonny gestured for Aleck to get in the front, and Liam hopped in the back next to Jack. Once they were all in, Jonny fired it up and they sped out.

As they got out onto the open road, Jonny switched the radio on. He always insisted on listening to crap Eighties tunes. Liam hated it so much.

"Aleck. I want you to listen to me. Deano is a decent lad, but he's too fucking headstrong. When Harry and I tell you to do something, you do it. You got that?"

"Yes, boss. Sorry, boss, we just thought you'd be pleased."

Liam shuddered. Just the "yes boss" would have done. Liam glanced at Jack, who looked worried too.

"I need lads who obey me to the letter, Aleck. I don't want you to surprise me unless it's my fucking birthday. Then you can surprise me with a bottle of scotch."

"Yes, boss," Aleck said. Liam detected a hint of nervousness in it this time.

"Good lad. You can help Harry with our new guest today. You do whatever he tells you."

"Me?"

Jonny patted him on the leg. "Yes, you. I'm giving you the chance to show me how you can obey the orders, no matter what they are."

They all remained silent for the rest of the journey. Things were panning out well. If Liam was surplus to requirements, Jonny might let him go home. Even though he would probably come across way too keen, he would give Marco a call. The thought of sleeping next to him again was too much to resist.

They drove through Jonny's gates and up the drive to his house. The van had got there before them. Harry stood on the gravel, waiting.

"Did he give you any trouble?" Jonny asked as they all got out.

"The usual struggling and threats. I had to slap him a few times," Harry replied.

"Fair enough. Won't hurt to soften him up a bit. Aleck here has volunteered to be your assistant today, Harold, my man," Jonny said, clapping a very nervous-looking Aleck on the shoulder.

"Good stuff," Harry said.

"What do you want us to do?" Liam asked, making sure Jonny wouldn't detect any hesitation from him.

"You got somewhere to be, hotshot?" Jonny asked.

"No, just wanted to make myself useful."

"Awww, is little Liam feeling left out?" Deano said, appearing from the side of the pool house.

"What have you been up to?" Jonny asked, narrowing his eyes.

"Nothing, boss. Just giving our friend a little pep talk. That's all."

There was blood on Deano's light grey hoodie cuffs.

"Jesus Christ. Do you never learn?" Harry said. "I told you to watch him."

Jonny stalked up to him. "I'm getting fucking sick of you. You can clean the pool house from top to toe. That will keep you busy. Jack, you can help him."

Jack sighed, but clearly didn't have the balls to argue. They both set off, bickering.

Jonny turned to Liam. "You go and watch the foreign twat while we talk tactics. If he talks, tell him the sooner he tells me everything, the quicker it will be over. But don't fucking touch him."

Jonny, Harry and Aleck went into the house. Liam walked round the side of the pool house. Jack and Deano were still arguing about who had to clean the toilets as he climbed the staircase that led to the attic.

They usually used it to keep the stock and anything else Jonny wanted to keep away from prying eyes.

It was dark and musty, and a figure sat up against the wall in the corner with his head down. Blood had spattered on the floor.

A flicker of recognition passed over Liam, making him stumble. Hand shaking, he flicked a switch, bathing the room in light.

The figure looked up and Liam's world went into freefall.

"*Marco?*"

Chapter Ten

"What the fuck?" Liam couldn't believe his eyes. How could Marco be here? Nausea swept over him as anxiety flooded his system.

"Liam? I could say the same thing," Marco retorted.

Frozen to the spot, Liam took in the injuries Deano had inflicted on Marco. They didn't look too bad. He had a cut above his eye and finger marks snaked around his neck. Thoughts swirled around Liam's mind about what the hell to do next. His heartbeat pounded in his ears as he tried to calm himself.

"You need to get me out of here," Marco pleaded, struggling against the rope that bound his wrists.

"I can't," Liam said. "They'll kill me."

Marco swallowed hard. "Listen to me and hear me properly. My uncle is big. He's got operations all over Italy, France and Spain. You are fucking with the wrong people if you stay with Wellingham, Liam."

"So that bit was true then? You do work for your uncle."

"We can have a dick-waving competition about who told the biggest lie when you get me out of here," Marco said. "We need to move quickly."

Liam's head spun out of control. This time last week, Marco would have been just another problem for Jonny and the gang to eliminate. But it was this week, and Liam couldn't just leave him. Could he? Indecision paralysed him. The connection between them could only be lust, surely.

"If you want me to fucking beg, then I will," Marco said. "The minute I give up why I'm here, they'll kill me. You know that and I know that. Either way, my uncle is coming. He will finish you all if I go missing. Help me and come with us. Please, Liam."

"Oi, Moseley."

Liam leapt out of his skin when he heard Jack's voice at the bottom of the stairs.

"What?" he called back, not taking his eyes off Marco.

"Boss wants you."

Liam stepped backwards towards the door.

"Don't do this, Liam. You and me together could be everything," Marco pleaded.

He couldn't take it and bolted from the room and down the stairs. "Keep an eye on him," he said to Jack, who was mopping the floor.

"Where's he going to go?" Jack sniggered.

"Just do it," Liam muttered.

Outside in the sunlight, he gulped in air and leant against the wall. How hadn't he picked up that Marco had been lying to him? Had he been so grateful for a scrap of kindness, he'd been blind to everything else? He tried to convince himself Marco had used him, but the look of desperation and need on Marco's face when he'd left him made the guilt stab at him.

Getting himself together, he walked around the patio to the main garden where he could hear voices. Jonny sat at the table with Harry, Aleck and Deano who had clearly left Jack to do the actual cleaning.

"All right?" Liam said, trying to sound as normal as possible. "Something up?"

"Those bitches Gina and Deb didn't show up last night. They're the sixth lot of girls who have gone over to that bastard up there. Fucking hell, I'm going to make him pay," Jonny roared, clenching his fists.

Liam thought he was going to pass out as the blood rushed to his head. Jonny Wellingham was capable of extreme violence when he was riled. Today, he was a ball of rage.

"Well, we have him now, boss," Harry said soothingly. "Things will go back to normal."

"Not good enough. I want it known that no one runs out on Jonny Wellingham for the chance of making a bit more cash. Ungrateful slags," Jonny snarled. "I'm going to make an example of them. I hope they've run a long way."

Liam sat down at the table and glanced nervously around.

"What you want me to do?" Deano asked.

"Kick the living shit out of them," Jonny shouted. "They won't be able to sell their pussies in a fucking dark room when you're through with them. You got it?"

Deano nodded.

An out-of-control Jonny made Liam terrified for Marco's fate. He couldn't stop thinking of him in the attic. He must be terrified.

"You want me to take Liam or Jack?" Deano asked.

"No. Pick up Steve and Tony on the way. I want my trusted lads up here. Go on, fuck off."

Deano got up from the table and headed for the front of the house. Jonny kept a few cars there for the lads to use.

"I want it slow. How dare he come here. The cheeky fucking bastard," Jonny raged. "You can do what you want with him when we've found that out."

Liam shuddered. In a way he was glad that Deano had gone. He was the only sick bastard that got enjoyment from this. Even so, Harry excelled at what he did and if Jonny wanted Marco to suffer, Harry would make sure he did.

"Are you about to start crying?" Jonny said to Liam.

"No, boss. I don't give a fuck," Liam said, trying to adopt a brave tone. "Just thinking about Claire. She never said anything about Gina and Deb."

"Tell that slut friend of yours if she gets any ideas, she'll know about it." Jonny turned to Harry. "You got everything?"

Harry nodded.

"Come on then," Jonny said. "Let's have him crying for the motherland."

They all got up from the table and made for the annex. Liam didn't know if his legs were going to be able to carry him to be a part of this. Jonny noticed him hanging back.

"What's up with you?" he yelled. "Something on the TV you'd rather watch? Move it."

Harry frowned at Liam. He had no choice. He slowly followed them out onto the front of the house. Just as they were crossing to go to the pool house, the electric gates at the bottom of the drive started to grind open.

"Who the fuck is that?" Harry said.

He squinted in the sunlight but could make out Sadie's pink Porsche Taycan driving towards them.

"Shit. Fuck," Jonny exclaimed. "I thought she was at her mother's."

"What are we going to do, boss?" Liam asked. He hoped this would buy Marco time while he got his head together.

"She's as nosey as her fucking mother," Jonny said. "I'm not having her seeing what we're up to and if that little poof starts screaming, she'll be all over us. Get rid of her, Liam. I don't care how you do it. Then come and tell me. We can soften him up a bit while we're waiting."

Jonny, Aleck and Harry marched over to the pool house. Liam had no idea what he would tell Sadie. She wasn't as stupid as Jonny seemed to think.

She pulled up next to him and leapt out.

"All right, Sadie?" he said.

"Where's my father?" she asked.

"He's out," Liam said. His mind racing, he tried to form a plan. Lying didn't come easily to him. He got flustered and panicky.

"That's a shit lie," Sadie said marching into the house.

Liam followed her. She slammed her keys down on the table in the hallway and spun around. God he would quite happily slap that smug little face. She always had been a spoilt little brat. Adulthood had only solidified it.

"Aren't you supposed to only come in here with an invitation?" she said. "Like a fucking vampire."

"You okay, Sadie?" Liam said. "You're spinning."

She sighed and threw her handbag down next to her keys.

"No, I'm fucking not. My bitch of a mother has announced that she's marrying that lowlife bloody bartender she's been shagging. There goes my inheritance. I want to speak to my father. He can do something about it."

Typical Sadie. Everything in her life had a price tag, even her mother's happiness. The bartender in question was on Jonny's payroll and had been handpicked by him. Jonny loathed his ex-wife, so Liam didn't fancy Sadie's chances at persuading him to help ruin the marriage.

"He's gone to try to find this new guy," Liam said. He couldn't get his mind off what was happening in the pool house. "He said he'll be back soon."

She sighed, checking her hair in the huge mirror. "Then why did I just see him at the top of the drive? Don't take me for a mug. You're so used to dealing with my father's army of halfwits you've forgotten how to handle a normal person."

She didn't mind living off the spoils of this foolish army. The entitlement that came from Sadie drove Liam mad.

"I meant he's going out in a minute," Liam continued. "He's really raging about this. I would leave it for now."

"I didn't ask your opinion," she spat. "Is he in that stinking pool house? I'll go myself."

She was about to leave when Liam grabbed her arm. "No, I'll get him for you."

"Take your hands off me," she said, wrestling her arm from his grasp. "Fine. Go and get him. But I'm waiting precisely five minutes, then I'm coming up there. That bloody woman is not going to waste all my birth right on some hired cock. I'll be in the living room. I need a drink."

"Got it."

Her Louboutin heels clacked on the marble floor as she stalked away. Liam ducked into the downstairs toilet. He grabbed his mobile phone and rang Claire.

"Twice in one day, I'm a lucky—"

"Shut up and listen to me. The other bloody gangster is Marco."

"Marco who?"

"Marco, Marco. The guy I told you about."

"Oh, *fucking hell*. What's happening? How do you know?"

"They've got him in the pool house. They're going to kill him, Claire."

"But—"

"Not just that. Jonny has found out about Gina and Deb. He's sent Deano and some lads to make an example of them. You need to warn them. Tell them to get the fuck out of Manchester and never come back."

Claire exhaled loudly on the other end of the phone. "Right. I'd better go and ring them."

"Claire, what am I going to do? I can't just stand there while they kill him. His uncle is some big fucking boss in Italy. They're taking over Manchester. He said he'll come whether he gets killed or not. They sound like nasty bastards."

"Jesus Christ, Liam. This is not good."

"And..."

"And what?"

"And I care for him, Claire. I really do. I didn't realise how much until I saw him in the attic. He's desperate."

"Let's think with our heads and not our dicks for a minute. Can you get him out of there?"

Liam had been trying to think of ways of getting Marco out without blowing his own cover. Every time he ran a blank. "Not without Jonny finding out I've been banging the other team."

"Who gives a fuck?" Claire retorted. "He's finished. If we side with this new gang, we're sitting pretty. Come on, let's think. I need to ring Gina quickly."

"If Jonny finds out I'm shagging Marco, he'll kill us both. You know what he's like about gay people."

Jonny had an innate hatred of anyone gay. He even stopped dealers in the lucrative Gay Village. Harry had established selling points on the edge of the area and Jonny still took the cash, but he wouldn't have a Wellingham Boy being seen in a gay bar.

"Then make the fucking jump, Liam."

"But my mum—"

"I haven't got time for this," Claire muttered, shutting him down. "You need to get him out. I don't know how you're going to do it, babe. But he can meet me at Victoria Station. I'll be there in twenty minutes."

"Then what?"

"I'll take him to Dolly's. She'll come good for us. She fucking hates Jonny."

Dolly Wishart had been one of Jonny's best madams. Five years ago, he'd sacked her saying he didn't want wrinkled old crows in his houses. He told her the customers wouldn't be able to get it up.

"How am I supposed to get him there?" Liam said. He had to fight the panic from setting in.

"I don't know. You're going to have to figure that out. I'm sorry, but Gina needs me."

The line went dead, and Liam stared at himself in the mirror. Trouble had followed him all the time he had been with Jonny but never this personally. He wanted to believe that his only reason was to be on the right side of a superior gang, but deep down he knew exactly why he was doing this. Something was happening between him and Marco and he didn't fully have an explanation for it. All Liam knew was he couldn't leave him to Jonny, Harry and the others. No matter what the consequences were. If he could do that and still stay innocent in Jonny's eyes, all the better.

He just had to think. Keeping as calm as possible, he flushed the toilet and went into the hall. His eyes were drawn to Sadie's bag and car keys on the table.

Suddenly a plan started to form.

He just hoped he wasn't too late.

Chapter Eleven

A blood-curdling cry came from the attic above as Liam dashed up the stairs two at a time. Coming into the attic, he saw Aleck standing over Marco. He held a pair of pliers aloft which to Liam's horror had a tooth in their vice-like grip. Harry stood behind the chair they had tied Marco to, holding his shoulders so he couldn't struggle.

"There's plenty more where that came from," Jonny said. He had a handful of Marco's hair and yanked his head back. "Who are you working for?"

Marco looked past Jonny and locked eyes with Liam. Blood poured from his mouth, but the faint glimmer of a smile washed over his face.

"Boss," Liam said.

"What the fuck is it?" Jonny shouted.

"Sadie is kicking off," Liam mumbled. "Something about her mother. She says if you're not down there in five minutes, she'll come up here."

Jonny had gone red again as if he were about to explode. "Why did you tell her I was here?"

"I didn't. She saw you," Liam said, sulkily. Marco still stared at him. Liam felt sure he would give the game away if he carried on like that. "What are you looking at?"

Jonny released Marco's hair. "I have to do everything round here." Jonny turned to Harry. "I'll get rid of her. Get the bath ready. Let's see how he fares with that. Strip him."

Jonny left them to it, cursing as he stomped down the stairs and slammed the outside door.

"You heard him," Harry said to Aleck. "Go and get the bath ready. Tell Jack we need tea towels."

Aleck threw the pliers down and he too left the room. The heat made the attic red-hot, Liam wanted to get out of there more than anything.

He just had to get rid of Harry now.

"You look like you're going to throw up," Harry said. "Not losing your bottle, are you?"

"He knows he's fucked," Marco said. Blood flecked on his lips as he spoke.

"No one asked you," Liam replied. He could hardly bring himself to look at Marco though. Harry stared at him strangely. Liam tried to reason with himself that the tension had made him paranoid.

"I hope you've got the bollocks to kill me," Marco continued. "Because you're going to have to. I'm not telling you shit. Your time on top is over, you small-town bastards."

Harry walked over to the door. "My balls are like steel, my little Italian friend. Don't you worry about that."

"Where are you going?" Liam asked.

"To make sure those feckless bastards are sorting things. Jonny will go off his head if he gets here and they haven't. Do you think you can manage to keep an eye on this one?"

Liam nodded and Harry left.

"Liam —"

He dashed over to Marco. "Shut up and listen. I'm going to loosen these, and we'll say you've got free. That dickhead Aleck has left his knife on the table over there. You walk me outside with it at my neck."

He could barely get the knots free but tore at them with a strength he didn't know he possessed.

"Then what?"

"I've left the keys to Sadie's car in the ignition. Get into town and meet Claire at Victoria Station. I've sent you a load of photos. Do you still have your phone?"

"It's at the flat. I'll go there first. I'll tell them I've been in a car accident. They won't have much trouble believing it, the state of me. You couldn't have thought of this before I lost a bloody tooth?"

Finally, the rope fell to the floor and Marco leapt to his feet. He went to kiss Liam, but Liam pushed him away.

"You're covered in blood. Just focus," Liam growled. "Hit me."

"What?" Marco said, looking confused.

"Fucking hit me and make it a good one."

Realisation dawned on Marco's face and quick as a flash he landed a punch squarely on Liam's jaw that sent him reeling across the room. He'd been hit before but not like that. It almost made him regret saying it.

"Fucking hell," he managed.

Once he'd righted himself, Marco had the knife to his throat and gripped his other arm. Even just that touch steadied Liam a little. Once again, he could smell Marco's cologne and it took him back to the apartment.

How perfect things had felt. He knew he was doing the right thing.

Marco had got himself in position in the nick of time as just at that moment, Harry appeared in the doorway. "What the fuck?"

"Not one step farther, you bastard," Marco said. "Clear the way for me or I'll slit his fucking throat."

Indecision seemed to plague Harry. For a split second Liam thought he was going to call their bluff. But finally, he went down the stairs.

"Let's do this," Liam whispered.

With the hand he'd wrapped round Liam's neck, Marco stroked him. The gentleness served to steady Liam, and they staggered down the stairs. Aleck, Jack and Harry were all outside the pool house. Each one of them looked as though they would gladly make a move at any moment.

Walking backwards, Marco dragged him across the gravel. Liam focused on staying upright. Just a few more steps and Marco would be free.

"Who the fuck let him out?" Jonny came out of the front door closely followed by Sadie.

"What's going on? Dad?"

"Get inside!"

"The fuck I will," she replied.

"If any of you come any closer, I'll slit him from ear to ear," Marco shouted.

Jonny stood in front of Sadie.

"Go on then," she shouted.

"Shut your mouth," Jonny barked.

They had reached Sadie's car. Marco opened the door. Liam glanced down and to his relief the keys he'd put there were still in place. It would be typical of Sadie to ruin the plan.

With an almighty shove, Marco sent Liam falling face-down in the gravel. Liam cried out as he grazed his face and rolled out of the way. Hands stinging, he managed to get to his feet just in time to see Marco slam the door shut.

"Dad. My car!" Sadie cried, dashing forward only to be grabbed by her father.

Marco fired the Porsche into life and slammed it into reverse, narrowly missing Liam Then he whacked it into first and zoomed down the drive. Not waiting for the gates to open, he smashed through them. Sadie let out a scream.

"Get after him," Jonny screamed.

"You'd better get me another one," Sadie whined.

Aleck and Jack ran to the van they had brought Marco in. Deano had taken the Mercedes. They would have no chance of catching a Porsche in the crap old van.

"Take the Volvo," Jonny shouted. "Do I have to tell you everything?"

Every second they lost gave Marco a better chance. Eventually, they did as they were told and set off down the drive.

"You okay?" Harry said walking over to him.

"Yeah. I think so."

Jonny stared at him. "What happened?"

"I don't know, boss. I was just standing there, and he went for me."

"Where did he get a knife from?" Jonny continued.

"I didn't properly see. He landed one on me and had got over to the table by the time I had got up. Maybe Aleck left it on there."

Jonny ran his hand through his thinning hair. "That useless tub of lard is getting on my last nerve. Harry.

Put him on security for one of the houses. I don't want to see his ugly little face again."

Harry nodded but seemed lost in thought.

"Who was he, Dad?" Sadie asked. "And what about my car?"

"I'll get you a new car. Fuck me, I need a drink."

Jonny stalked into the house, closely followed by Sadie. Liam tentatively touched his jaw. Marco had hit him pretty hard, and it hurt to speak.

"Come on," Harry said. "We'd better get you cleaned up."

"It wasn't my fault, Harry. Honest." He didn't like the way Harry still stared at him.

"I know that, lad. So does the boss. That's why you're not on the way to join Davey in the quarry. Come on. We'll find you a scotch in the pool house."

Liam followed Harry. He hoped he had done enough for Marco. It felt as though he were falling down a whirlpool. If anyone saw Claire at the station, he would be in for it. But he couldn't leave. He just couldn't.

* * * *

"That bitch would have let him kill me for her car."

"And that surprises you in what way? Hold still."

Harry dabbed damp cotton wool on his face, trying to draw the little bits of gravel out. It stung like hell and his jaw made speaking pretty painful.

Jack hadn't done much of a job at cleaning the snooker room. Liam took a swig of the scotch that Harry had given him. He hated the stuff, but he needed something to calm his nerves. "At least the boss doesn't blame me. You don't think he does, do you?" he asked.

He had begun babbling but hoped they'd put it down to a near death experience.

"What could you do?" Harry asked. "Although I've no fucking idea how he got free. I tightened those ropes myself."

Liam flinched as Harry dabbed him with the cotton wool. "He's got a decent right hook on him," he said, hoping he had convinced Harry of their plan.

"I'm surprised he could bring himself to do it."

"What do you mean?" Liam asked. Alarm bells rang full peal, and he suddenly realised he'd made a mistake staying here.

Harry went over and closed the French windows. Dread began to gnaw at Liam. What was going on?

"Level with me. You know him. What's the situation?" Harry asked. He slumped down in the chair opposite Liam. He seemed tired.

"Of course I don't know him. What you on about?" Liam replied.

"Liam. You're a good lad but you're a shit liar. Now I can go and tell Jonny what I suspect, but no doubt we'll have to pick up with you where we left off with him. I don't want to do that. Not to you. But I will if I have to."

The silence in the room felt oppressive. Liam began to think he should have just got in the car with Marco like Claire said. "Harry, honest—"

Harry started to get up. Liam thought about the bath in the next room, still full of water. The chair upstairs. The pliers. He had no choice but to go out on a limb. "I didn't know, all right? I met him the other night. We...well, we..."

Settling in his seat, Harry stared hard at Liam. "I should have known. You've never been like the other lads, have you? They go through girls like water. I can't remember you ever showing any interest."

Liam couldn't meet his gaze. The moment he had dreaded for the last ten years had finally arrived. "Neither have you," he said meekly.

"I know better. You're too young for that. Did he know who you work for?"

"Of course not. It was as much a shock to him as me."

"Fucking hell," Harry said. "This is a right mess. Do you know where he's gone?"

"No idea," Liam lied. "I just said I'd get him out of here. He means nothing to me."

It was as though the room had shrunk and Harry's stare might as well have been a probe going straight into Liam's mind.

"Why didn't you run with him?"

"I told you, he doesn't mean anything."

Harry's face was blank. "You went out on a limb for someone that means nothing? That's bullshit and you know it."

"Fine. What if Mum comes back?" Liam said, eventually.

"Your mum? Are you kidding me? Is that why you've stuck around all these years?"

Liam nodded miserably.

"Liam, your mother isn't coming back. That I can guarantee you."

"She might."

"She won't. Take it from me. Jesus what a bloody day this is turning out to be. You know what Jonny is like about queers. If he gets wind about you, you're fucked."

Liam shook his head. "He wouldn't. Jonny knows I've been loyal all these years."

Harry slammed his hand on the arm of the chair. It made Liam jump and he stared at him.

"Let me tell you a little story about what loyalty means to Jonny Wellingham. About fifteen years ago, long before you came along, there was a guy called Lorenzo de Luca. You remind me a bit of him. Skinny and loyal. He'd run with Jonny since the early days. In fact, me, him and Jonny rose up the ranks of the old Ancoats Gang together. We made a pact early on that we would take the city as a team."

Liam frowned. He had never heard this name before.

"Then Jonny made his move on old Si Belmont. He finished him once and for all. Poor bastard didn't see it coming. We took the city from then on. The bloody lot. We were fucking flying."

"What happened to Lorenzo?" Liam asked quietly.

Harry drained his glass. "He got too trusting of our Mr Wellingham. Stupid bastard let slip he was queer, didn't he? He thought no one could touch him, but the boss had different ideas. He didn't want that in his gang, so he framed him for stealing the stock and selling it on the side."

Liam frowned. "So, he ran him out of town?"

"No, Liam. He had some lads take him to Chorlton Water Park and put a load of lead in him. They left his body floating down the Mersey. No one ever heard Lorenzo de Luca again."

"But things change," Liam said, desperately.

Harry leant forward. "Give me one indication that Jonny has changed. Just one."

Liam got up and paced over to the French doors. Through them he could see Jonny and Sadie arguing through the kitchen window. His world crashed in on him.

"What am I supposed to do then?"

"If I was you, I'd give up this new bastard. He's trouble. I don't know what it is about him, but this is personal. Then let them fight it out. Just run, Liam. Go to Shaun or something."

Liam thought about his brother in Blackpool. They had a strained relationship. Shaun didn't approve of him working for Jonny.

"But what about Mum?"

"Jesus fuck, lad. Your mum isn't a part of this. Get it into your thick head. She's gone."

Liam had spent so many nights in this room. It wasn't all bad being with Jonny. He could be one of the most generous people in the world. His barbecues were legendary, and he'd picked Liam up when he had nowhere else to go. This had been the family he'd never had.

But Marco had made him feel like he had a place in the world. When he'd held him as sleep wrapped itself around him, Liam had felt safe for the first time in his life. Really, truly safe.

"I don't think I can give him up, Harry," Liam said.

"Then you'd better run."

Chapter Twelve

Walking as fast as his legs would carry him down Jonny's drive, Liam half expected to hear a shout behind him. But Harry had been true to his word and let him run. Stepping through the mangled gates at the bottom, Liam stared at the mansion.

Something told him he would never see it again. The next step, out onto the street, would probably be the biggest one he'd ever make. He dithered for a minute, thinking about all the years he had belonged to Jonny Wellingham. It felt like such a big move for Liam, but on the other side waited a man who Liam was falling for. He could admit that now. Also, his best friend in the whole world had jumped in to help and she would kick his arse if he didn't show up at some point. So, he took a deep breath and walked briskly down the road.

It was a straight bus route into town from Jonny's, but once Claire had messaged to say that Marco had made it safely to Dolly's, Liam took buses all over town. For two reasons, really. One, he had the paranoid feeling that someone might have followed him.

Secondly, he needed to get his head together. Being surrounded by normal people leading their safe lives gave him a chance to focus.

Being a Jonny Wellingham Boy meant he was no stranger to drama like today, but he'd never had feelings for any of it. Early on, Harry had taught him how to disconnect from the horrors that sometimes lay before them. They were all for the greater good.

Eventually he got out at Salford Precinct and walked through the ancient back streets until he stood looking up at Woolton Towers, a dismal Sixties tower block standing at the exact spot where the two cities of Salford and Manchester met.

It matched about ten others — the ones closer to town had had a facelift but this was off the beaten track. Liam had been here once before, a couple of years ago, when Dolly had held a party to celebrate her fiftieth birthday. Jonny had sent a case of prosecco and a huge bag of weed. *Little did she know that would be her severance pay.*

He buzzed through the intercom and, like a scene from a sci-fi movie, the doors opened on their own and he walked through. His heart pounded as the lift took him up to Dolly's floor. A strong smell of urine made his eyes water, and someone had scraped *What is the point?* into the metal doors. He was a far cry from the bergamot-fragranced lift of Marco's posh apartment.

Marco.

He had looked furious that Liam had even dithered about helping him. Marco was obviously part of something bigger than Wellingham's little gang. He was probably used to total loyalty. He might not want to see him. In which case, all of this would have been for nothing, and Liam would be on the run alone.

Not alone. Claire wouldn't forsake him. His Plan B was for him and Claire to leg it to Blackpool. Shaun would be furious with him but he'd let him lie low for a bit. At last, he stood at Dolly's door and knocked.

"Here he is," Dolly said, beaming as she answered. "Come on in, love."

Dolly was one of those women to whom glamour bordered on a religion. She had been Manchester's highest-paid sex worker in the nineties, and she still made sure every detail was perfect. Rumour had it that she kept a few high-profile regulars, but Dolly would never confirm or deny it. With her platinum-blonde hair piled up on her head and her hourglass figure sheathed in a bright pink maxi dress, she looked fabulous.

She threw her arms around him. "You've had quite a day, my love."

Liam fought the tears which threatened to overpower him as he relaxed into her hug. "Are they here?"

She gestured for him to walk down the narrow landing and into the lounge. There he found Claire, lying on a big floral sofa with a joint in her hand. When she saw Liam, she leapt up and dashed over, flinging her arms around him.

"Oh, thank God."

She held him tight and this time the tears did come. The familiar smell of her was too much and they just stood there for a second.

They broke apart and Liam scanned the room. "Where is he?"

"He's having a lie down," Claire said, staring at him. "They worked him over. Looks like they had a go at you too. What happened?"

Liam rubbed his jaw. "Marco. I told him to be convincing. No bloody point after all that."

Dolly rubbed his back. "Go down the way you came, second door on the right."

Liam nodded. "Thank you so much. You will never know how grateful I am."

Dolly waved him away and settled down on the sofa.

Now he had got there, apprehension overwhelmed him. He could easily have run straight out again. Instead, he walked down the landing to the door and gently pushed it open. The early evening sunlight forced its way around the badly fitting blinds and Liam could just make out the sleeping figure in the bed.

He stepped out of his trainers and lowered himself carefully down on the bed. Marco moved in his sleep. Liam froze but then managed to mould his body around him. He snaked his hand over Marco's hips and buried his face in the curls. That was when his whole body relaxed.

He was home.

Marco turned and stared into Liam's eyes. Liam winced when he saw the bruises on Marco's face.

He went to say something, but Marco's lips silenced him. Liam let the emotion rush over him, and he returned the kiss...gently, because his jaw still throbbed. Even so, it was the best kiss he had ever had in his life.

Slowly he broke away. He could hear the television in the next room and people in the flat above were arguing about something, but it could have been a million miles away.

Silently they undressed. Liam ran his hands down the bruises on Marco's chest. Anger rose in him that people he had classed as friends had done this. Being on the other side of Wellingham's Boys felt very different and very scary.

Naked, they melded their bodies together. It had to be more than passion—it felt like they were forging something important. Liam kissed him again. Marco might be muscle-bound and the best-looking man he had ever seen, but Liam wanted to protect him.

They lay there for a while, Marco's head nestled in the crook of Liam's neck, Liam stroking his back while Marco held on to him.

Right then, Liam made a vow to himself that he would never let anyone hurt this man again. *Not ever.*

"You owe me a tooth," Marco said.

"I'm so sorry I waited," Liam replied. "I panicked."

Marco hugged him tightly. "What changed your mind?"

The million-dollar question. The one that had swirled around Liam's brain for most of the bus routes in Manchester. But he had fixed on a plan of how to deal with this and he was determined to go through with it. "Because I think I'm falling for you."

The silence stretched like an eternity. It had been quite a day so he might as well put it out there. The time for lying had passed.

"That's handy," Marco said at last. "Because I think I feel the same."

The nervous tension that had engulfed Liam's body ever since he'd walked into that attic and seen Marco tied up simply floated away. His body ached from being tensed for hours, but now that was replaced by a lightness.

Marco leant up and kissed him again, hard. He moved his body so that he straddled Liam. Taking hold of Liam's hands, he tentatively explored his mouth with his tongue. Liam winced as a sharp shock of pain shot up from his jaw.

Marco frowned at him. "I socked you good, didn't I?"

Liam smiled. "Remind me never to get on the wrong side of you."

"I don't have a wrong side for you, Liam Moseley."

"Cheesy."

"This is a cheesy moment. It's fine."

He kissed him again and Liam went to hug him. This time Marco winced.

"Do you need a doctor?" Liam asked.

"No, nothing I can't handle. Dolly gave me the once over. There is nothing broken. Except maybe my spirit."

"I can fix that," Liam replied, snuggling into him.

Marco leant down and kissed his neck. "We can fix each other," he murmured in his ear.

"Are we going to do this?" Liam asked. He ran his hands through Marco's curls. He loved the soft feeling of them.

"All the way, baby," Marco replied.

Ignoring the pain, Liam kissed him, running his tongue over the gap left by the tooth. He hated that they would have a reminder of this terrible day.

Marco was hard now, and Liam reached down, stroking his cock. Marco groaned into his mouth. Liam knew it wasn't from pain, but from desire.

His own cock had hardened too, and Marco crawled down his body. Feeling Marco's breath on him sent Liam into orbit. Gently, he blew up the length of Liam's hard-on. They had been here before but this time felt like more than sex. It was as though they were committing to something. But Liam would bet neither of them knew what it was. When Marco took him in his mouth and the heat set his cock ablaze, Liam knew he would do anything for this man.

Liam felt so close to Marco as he watched him. Marco stroked his leg gently, letting his fingers creep down to his balls. They contracted at his touch, sending goosebumps all over Liam's body.

He sat up, letting his cock fall out of Marco's mouth and pulling him up into a kiss. Wrapping his legs around Marco's waist to balance them, Liam reached down and took hold of Marco's dick. He lightly ran his fingers over the head before squeezing the base. Marco closed his eyes and sighed.

"*Si, piccolo.*"

Liam massaged it, running his clenched palm up and down. Marco took hold of Liam's cock in response and they kissed again

Liam never wanted it to stop, but soon his orgasm began to build. He wrapped his free arm around Marco's shoulder and their foreheads touched. "Oh, yeah."

Marco sped up, as did Liam, their mouths inches away from each other,

"Oh fuck," Marco grunted.

He came in thick spurts that fell onto Liam's hand and cock. Liam soon followed him. Still gripping Marco's neck, he thrust his lips onto his. He let the judders flow through his body as he lost himself in yet another kiss.

Once his heartrate had returned to normal, Marco leant down and picked up his T-shirt. He cleaned them both and threw it on the floor. "I guess that sealed the deal," he said with a wink.

"More fun than a handshake," Liam replied.

He flopped back on the bed and held his arm out for Marco, who snuggled into him.

"I fit perfectly in here," Marco said, kissing his chest.

"I wanted to kill them for what they did to you. I promise you I will never let anyone do that to you again," Liam said.

"Don't make promises like that, Liam. In our game, you can't keep them."

They lay there for what could have been hours. Liam had totally lost track of time.

"I thought I would never lie with you like this again," Marco said eventually. "I'm not ashamed to say I was shitting it for a moment there."

"I can't believe that we actually woke up together today. It's been a fucker of a day," Liam replied.

"You're right. I feel like we've fitted a week in a day. Your friend Claire is nice. She speaks very highly of you."

Liam frowned. "Have you been getting the lowdown on me?"

"We had to while away the hours until your appearance," Marco replied. "You have a good friend there. You have nothing to worry about."

"She's the best," Liam said. "We've been through a lot together. I couldn't do any of this without her."

It must have been dusk outside because the room had grown dark.

"I suppose we should think about what to do next," Marco said.

He was right, but if it was up to Liam, he would stay in bed and shut the rest of the world out. One day they would build a place that was just for them. Liam had never had a home. Maybe he had a chance now. "What first?"

"I'd better ring my uncle. He will be angry with me," Marco said. "I wasn't supposed to go quite so far as I did."

Marco sounded like a little boy when he spoke about his uncle. It intrigued Liam. "Tell me about him. I really don't fancy getting caught up with Rome's version of Jonny Wellingham."

Marco laughed loudly and sat up, so he knelt facing Liam. "My uncle is nothing like Jonny bloody Wellingham. On that you have my word."

"How old is he?"

"In his forties. He is my mother's brother and he's tough but fair. Not like Wellingham, who is just a pig."

Liam frowned. "You know a lot about Jonny."

"I do my homework."

"I bet Jonny is furious right now," Liam said with a shudder. He wondered who would be getting it in the neck. He hoped Deano. That was when he realised he hadn't even asked about Gina and Deb.

"Come on," he said, making to get up. "We have to show our faces."

Marco pinned him down and planted a kiss on him.

"I'm going to take Jonny Wellingham down, Liam. You know that don't you?"

Liam nodded. He also knew that wherever this vendetta would take Marco, Liam would be by his side. They had jumped together now. The only way out was to finish Jonny before he finished them.

"Not quite. *We're* going to take him down," he replied.

Chapter Thirteen

"Oh, look who's come up for air," Claire said when Liam walked into the lounge.

The all-too-familiar blush burned across his face.

"Leave the lad alone," Dolly told her. "If I had a handsome Italian to crawl into bed with, you wouldn't see me for days."

"Where is Casanova?" Claire asked.

"He's ringing his uncle," Liam said, sinking down on the sofa next to her.

Dolly sat in the chair by the window, smoking. "The big gangster who's going to finish Jonny Wellingham," she mused. "Now this is going to be worth seeing."

Dolly's lounge had been expensively decorated. It seemed strange because the high rise wasn't exactly the Ritz. Claire and Liam sat on an overstuffed floral sofa and Dolly's chair was bright yellow. They both clashed with the purple rug and mustard walls, but somehow it all worked.

Liam wondered why she stayed here if she had done so well for money. "I meant to ask you," he said to Claire. "What about Gina and Deb?"

Claire passed him a joint and stretched out, putting her feet in his lap. "They got away. Thanks to you."

"I'm a regular saviour today, aren't I?"

Dolly stubbed her cigarette out and set about rolling them another joint. "Don't you put yourself down, young man. You've made a massive step today. But the right one. That's the main thing."

Hearing it from someone as experienced as Dolly felt reassuring. Something he needed at that moment.

Marco came into the room and stood in the doorway awkwardly.

"Come on in," Dolly said with a warm glow about her. "How are you feeling?"

"Still a bit sore," he said.

Marco sat down on the floor with his back to Liam who couldn't resist reaching out and stroking those curls. Claire caught his eye and gave him a wink.

"How was your uncle?" Liam asked.

"He's not happy with me," Marco replied. "I wasn't supposed to make a move. I was just meant to set up the stock, sound out some supply lines and wait until he could get here."

Liam put his hand on Marco's shoulder. "You've done pretty well setting up supply without Jonny hearing about it."

"I brought a van load with me," Marco said. "When I realised how tight he's got this place sewn up, I wanted to fuck things up first. But Uncle Z won't listen. He thinks I've acted too hastily and shown our hand."

"Where are you keeping it?" Claire said. "Not in the posh flat, surely."

"As if," Marco replied. "I keep moving the van around. It's in the car park of the flats at the moment."

"Fucking hell, you're taking a risk, aren't you?" Dolly said. "You should have listened to your uncle though. Taking that piece of shit for everything won't be easy."

"It's taking so bloody long and I wanted to show him... Well, after Naples," Marco said.

Dolly lit the joint and exhaled loudly. "What happened in Naples?"

Marco sighed. "I fucked up royally. Some stupid copper in Venice found out we had her boss on the payroll. So, we dealt with her, although we didn't finish the job and two bloody tourists led us on a merry dance all the way to frigging Naples."

"Did you sort it?" Claire asked.

"I sent in a load of our best. But the police got there just after us. The ones that weren't killed are in prison. Wiped out so many of Uncle Z's men. He's having to recruit pretty bloody quickly, or we'll lose everything. That's why he sent me here. To start making some cash and to get out of his sight for a bit."

Dolly handed him the joint. "Oh dear, and now you've screwed up again."

"Exactly," Marco said taking a drag. "I'm about as popular as a dose of the clap."

"You haven't exactly fucked up," Claire said. "You've still got the stock and the girls. We just need to lie low until your uncle's reinforcements arrive, then its bye bye, Jonny."

She rubbed her hands with glee as she said this.

"She's a bloodthirsty little madam," Dolly laughed. "Although Jonny Wellingham has it coming, the bastard. You'll stay here for a bit. This is the safest place for you."

"Are you sure, Doll?" Claire asked.

"Course I am. We have systems in this tower. If we need to get out, you trust in Dolly."

Liam relaxed for the first time in forever. Then he sat up. "I don't have any clothes or anything. What am I going to do?"

"Well, you can't go home to your flat," Claire said. "Deano or Harry will have turned that place over already."

Settling down, Liam realised that he didn't have a thing to his name now except for the clothes he had on. He thought about his PlayStation and trainers. He'd bet that Deano had laid claim to them.

"Don't worry," Marco said, handing him the joint. "I packed a bag at the flat when I got my phone. We've got plenty of stuff."

"You'll have to fill out a bit if you're going to fit his stuff," Claire teased. "Press-ups at dawn, pipsqueak."

Liam nipped her toe. He knew that Marco was in far better shape than him, but he didn't care. He would be falling asleep in those muscular arms tonight and for many other nights if he had anything to say about it.

* * * *

The night turned into days. They fell into a decent routine. Dolly would go out and get the shopping and they would take it in turns to cook. Marco got the best reviews, recreating dishes from Italy that rivalled the pasta he had cooked Liam for their first proper meal together.

When they weren't watching Dolly's seemingly endless collection of old movies, they would play games or just chat. At night, Liam and Marco relished their alone time. Happiness had never been familiar to Liam but he guessed that this was what it was like.

It was a temporary happiness though, and they would have to make a move at some point. Whatever they did, Jonny would be waiting.

One morning, Dolly came into the lounge, putting her mobile phone in the pocket of her housecoat.

"You kids are going to have to make yourselves scarce this afternoon. I've got a punter."

Liam was painting Claire's toenails a lurid pink she had found in Dolly's bedroom. Marco was using her laptop, flicking through estate agent webpages.

He looked up. "I thought we said no visitors."

"You're not the boss of Manchester yet," Dolly said, sitting opposite him at the table. "Randolph is one of my oldest clients."

"Randolph?" Liam said, catching Claire's eye and giggling.

"Randolph Buckingham if you must know," Dolly said, drawing her housecoat together.

Claire lifted her head. "The local councillor?"

"The very same." Dolly sniffed. "Been coming to see me for twenty years. He's running for parliament soon, he reckons. Imagine the contacts there. It could set me up for life. You lot will have to stay in the spare room."

Claire leant back, making a face. "Liam and Marco's sex palace? Lucky me."

"Shut it," Liam said. "You're only jealous."

"I bloody am. How about you take a walk on the wild side with me, Marco? It will pass the time."

Marco gave her a sickly-sweet smile. "I take a walk on that side every night. Don't I, Liam?"

"Don't make him blush," Dolly chided. "Chuck us that nail varnish over. Randy likes me in pink."

"Randy," Claire said, dissolving into fits of giggles.

"You'd better not take the piss when he gets here," Dolly said. "He's a good payer. Bloody weird stuff, but after all these years, who am I to judge?"

Liam finished Claire's last toe and got up, gently placing them on a cushion. He passed the nail varnish to Dolly and stood behind Marco, massaging his shoulders.

On the screen was an old farmhouse for lease.

"What's that?" Liam asked.

"Ah-ha. This is the new base for us. When I rang Uncle Z the other night, he told me to get cracking on this part of the plan, at least. He wants somewhere we can easily guard and a bit out of town. This place is perfect."

It might have been a bit dated, but it made Liam's heart dance. Slap-bang in the middle of the country, there was nothing but fields and woods surrounding. They would be able to see anyone approaching for miles around. It could be the place Liam had been dreaming of that would give them the safety they desperately needed.

"Our own castle," Liam said, kissing the top of his head.

"You two make me want to puke." Claire lit a cigarette.

"Aww, I think they're sweet," Dolly said. "I'll miss you when you're gone. It's been fun in a weird, are-we-going-to-die way."

She was right. It had been nice. Liam thought that when he had spent the day with Marco in the posh flat, they had created a bubble. But here they were creating a future. They had a long way to go but it seemed different. He had always been a passenger and he wasn't under any illusions that Marco was in the driving seat at the moment, but Liam liked being listened to and respected. "What time is Randy coming?"

"Not until two."

"I'll make us some lunch then," Marco said, shutting the laptop and getting up.

Liam's heart danced when Marco kissed him.

"Not for me you won't," Dolly said, inspecting her left-hand nails. "You've been fattening me up for bloody Christmas. I'll never get into that corset."

"Claire?" Marco asked.

She sat up, pressing her nails to see if they were drying. "Too right. I've been thinking you know," she said. "I might quite fancy a more managerial role when your Italian chums arrive. I'm sick of working shifts."

Dolly lit a cigarette. "You could do a lot worse than our Claire. She's got her head screwed on, that one."

Marco looked to Liam who shrugged.

"Well, I do owe you one," Marco said. "Let's talk about it."

They talked about nothing else over the meal. Claire had a determined soul when she put her mind to something. True to her word, Dolly had a lunch of cigarettes and wine while the others dug into yet another amazing pasta creation from Marco.

Liam had lost track of time when the buzzer made them all jump.

"Fucking hell," Dolly exclaimed, stubbing her cigarette out in the overflowing ashtray. "He's here. In the spare room now, all of you. He'll have to take me in a negligee. I'm never getting into the corset now. Fuck."

Giggling like children, they grabbed the bottle of wine and scuttled into the spare room. They all fell down onto the bed in time to hear muffled voices on the landing.

"Politicians are dirty bastards," Claire whispered. "I had one that insisted I dress as a nun. When did boring sex go out of fashion?"

"They can get that at home, I guess," Marco said.

"Yeah, I suppose," she agreed, taking a healthy glug from the wine bottle.

Dolly had taken Randolph into the lounge. Her bedroom lay in between the two rooms so they could at least talk without fear of being overheard.

"How much longer until your uncle's men get here?" Claire asked.

Liam almost didn't want them to come. It might be fun making plans but bringing them to fruition was a whole different ballgame. After the events at Jonny's house, he had enjoyed not taking risks for once.

"Another couple of days. He's sending my cousins, Enzo and Giovanni."

Claire fluffed her hair. "Enzo and Giovanni, eh? Maybe I should get myself a sexy Italian too."

"Enzo is one of us," Marco said. "But Giovanni is a good-looking chap. A bit old for you though."

"I don't mind older," Claire said. "They're grateful."

Liam shook his head. "You're terrible."

"Giddy up, you fucking bastard," Dolly shouted. Then the crack of a whip sounded throughout the flat.

"What the hell?" Liam said.

They buried their faces in the duvet so their cackles couldn't be heard.

"I know she said he had odd tastes, but what on earth is going on in there?" Marco said, wiping his eyes.

"Hey, I've had a thought," Claire said.

"Uh-oh," Liam replied.

"If he wins the election, he would be worried shitless about what people think. What if we got a photo?" Claire said. "You never know when we might need a favour higher up."

"Dolly would kill us," Liam said. "Seems harsh when she's been so decent."

"Leave Dolly to me. I bet we wouldn't have to do anything with it anyways. He would cack himself at the very thought."

"It's not a bad idea," Marco said. "In Italy we have all sorts on the payroll. Comes in very handy."

"See? Told you I had managerial tendencies," Claire said, proudly.

Liam reached into his pocket and took out his phone.

"Another circuit, Randy," Dolly shouted.

They all collapsed into fits of giggles again.

"We need to get a hold of ourselves if we're going to do this," Liam said.

"Come on, then," Claire said, getting off the bed.

Holding on to one another, they pulled open the door. Down the other end of the landing, the lounge door was ajar.

Slowly they crept towards it. Liam got there first and peered through the crack. He could see a portly man in his sixties, stark naked with Dolly in her fuchsia-pink satin negligee astride his back, holding a riding crop.

The man crawled around the lounge and judging by the erection on him, he was having a whale of a time.

Claire and Marco were sniggering over his shoulder as he raised the phone up to get a photo. He clicked a few, but then Randolph changed direction, so he faced the door.

They all froze as he saw them.

"What on earth?"

Dolly blazed incandescent with rage. Randolph struggled to his feet and sent her flying onto the floor.

"Who are you?" he exclaimed.

They bolted back to the spare room. Claire was giggling but Marco had worry written all over his face.

"What if he recognised us?" Marco said.

"Of course he wouldn't."

They heard raised voices in the lounge and in record time, Randolph stormed down the landing.

"After twenty years, I thought I could trust you, Dolly."

"You can, Randy. Honestly. I have my niece and her friends staying. I didn't want to say because I missed you. Don't be sore."

"Sore? I'm *furious*. I'm sorry, Dolly, but without trust there isn't anything. What if my wife finds out?"

Claire shook her head. "Hypocritical fat fuck."

The door slammed, making them all jump. Then the spare room door opened, and a furious Dolly stood there. "Living room. Now."

They all trudged behind Dolly like a repentant conga and sat on the sofa in a line with their heads bowed as she lit up a cigarette.

"I've put my neck on the line for you ungrateful little bastards."

"Dolly…" Liam started. He hated seeing her so angry.

"No. I'm not having it. You're bang out of order. That is my retirement fund that you've sent packing. What the fuck do you think I'm going to do now? You kids have all your lives ahead of you. I can't quite see me shelf stacking, can you?"

"I promise you won't have to do that," Marco said.

"Oh, and I suppose your wonderful uncle is going to buy me an island, is he? Well in case it had escaped your notice, the plans you've made this week are just that. Plans." Dolly took a deep drag on her cigarette and ran her hands through her hair. "Jesus Christ, what am I doing? I should have told you to sling your hook when I heard Jonny was involved. I swore I'd never get caught up with that louse again."

"That blubbering bag of wind won't say anything," Claire said. "You heard him. He's terrified of wifey finding out."

Dolly's phone rang.

"That had better be him or you owe me a fuck-ton of money, Marco Ponti," Dolly said walking over to the dining table. "Ugh, it's Teresa from downstairs. What does she bloody want?"

With her bright pink talons, she pressed the buttons on the ancient phone. Liam didn't dare catch the eye of Marco or Claire.

"Teresa. I'm in the middle of something at the moment—"

The way she stopped speaking made them all look up. Her expression was one of abject fear.

"Right," she said. "Ring the girls. Tell them we're running."

She finished the call and slammed the phone down.

"They're here."

Chapter Fourteen

None of them spoke as they dashed through the flat. Luckily Marco had insisted they be ready to run at any opportunity and they had left packed bags in the cupboard in the hall.

Dolly slipped on her trainers. In any other circumstances it would have been funny to see her running around in a pink negligee and trainers, but not today. Fear crackled up Liam's neck as she stood. The woman clearly meant business.

"Follow me," Dolly said. "The ladies of this tower won't let us down."

They ran out of the flat and to the lift. But the display told them it was already on its way up. They were too late.

"What are we going to do?" Liam gasped.

"The stairs, now," Dolly commanded.

They ran in a line after her. Claire, then Marco followed by Liam. Two flights down and voices could be heard coming from below. Liam glimpsed figures running up the steps.

"Shit," Claire said. "We're trapped."

But Dolly simply shook her head and led them onto the landing. She gave a strange knock on the door of a flat that would be directly under hers. A woman of around the same age as Dolly answered it and wordlessly let them in.

"Is it Jonny?" she whispered to Dolly, who only nodded in return. "Jesus Chris, Doll. I don't know what you're mixed up in, but Martha's ready. That little fucker should be taken down a peg or two."

Footsteps sounded as they made their way onwards on the stairs. In the distance above them were bangs and crashes. It sounded like Jonny had set his lads loose on Dolly's home.

"I'll go and clean up after you've gone, love," the woman said, patting Dolly's shoulder.

"Thanks, Brenda. You're a good friend," Dolly said. Even so, she looked devastated that her sanctuary was being ripped apart. Liam wanted to grab her and hold her, but they needed to stay focused.

Satisfied there weren't any others coming up the stairwell, Brenda opened the door and let them out.

They ran down another two flights,

"It's them," came a voice from above.

Terror ran up Liam's spine as he heard heavy footsteps following them down the stairs. He didn't dare look up. If his nerve left him, he was fucked.

"Don't worry, loves," Dolly said. Her face suggested they still had a chance. Liam marvelled at her courage. Her life was being ripped apart yet she remained totally together. He wasn't sure he could be like that if he were in her position.

Once again, they headed out onto the landing and to a flat across the way. Dolly repeated her knock and an elderly lady with a face full of makeup answered.

"Come on," she said with a chuckle. "What are you up to now?"

They squeezed through her door and stood with their backs against the landing. Marco had his ear to the door. The shouts didn't just pass by this time. They were outside.

Liam nodded to the spyhole and Marco stared through. They hardly dared breathe as they tried to make out what the muffled voices were saying.

Holding up two fingers, Marco seemed ready to attack but Liam put a hand on his arm and silently shook his head.

Jonny would have come mob-handed. Stealth was their only chance of getting out of this alive. Attack would have to wait for another day.

This flat sat on the second floor. They were nearly there. Claire mimed to Martha that they would go into the lounge. She nodded and they all carefully tiptoed through. In here the television blared but they could talk without worrying they'd be heard. The room was totally different to Dolly's, with a cheap brocade three-piece suite and pictures of kittens on the wall. The flat had an overwhelming smell of lavender.

"Has he put them on there as sentries do you think?" Claire whispered.

"I reckon so," Marco said. "He knows we're still in here, which means there's someone on the door."

"I'll find out for you," Martha said.

"You can't," Dolly said.

"I was working for harder men than him while Jonny Wellingham was shitting in his nappies," she said with a wink. "They'll be stoned anyway. You kids always are."

"Can't we jump?" Liam asked.

Dolly shook her head. "I'd like to see you outrun him with a broken leg, you silly little fool. This isn't the bloody movies."

Martha had her coat on and strode purposefully over the room to pick up a walking stick behind the sofa. They followed her to the door, and she took on the guise of a decrepit old woman.

"What are you two doing out here?" she said walking out and gently closing the door behind her.

They pressed their ears to the door with Marco staring through the spyhole.

"Piss off, you old crow."

It was Steve. Liam thanked his lucky stars it wasn't Deano.

"Cheeky so-and-so," Martha replied. "I've a good mind to ring the coppers."

"And I'll wring your bloody neck," Steve replied. "Go on, fuck off."

The wait seemed to last forever, but soon enough Dolly's phone vibrated. She pulled it out of the mac she had hastily thrown on when they had left her flat and read the message. Silently she held up three fingers.

There were three at the main door. Dolly nodded to go through into Martha's living room.

"Right. There's two out there and three downstairs," she said. "We need to act fast. Once they realise there's nothing to find in my place, they will be everywhere. Fucking Randolph must have tipped them off. Well, I'm done with him now. Easiest bit of money I ever made and now it's all fucked up."

"We need a diversion," Liam said.

Dolly made a call. "Brenda? Help us out, love."

In no time, they heard a commotion upstairs and a cry of pain. They dashed to the front door and this time Liam pressed his eye to the spyhole. Steve and whoever had been put with him could be seen running towards the staircase door. To Liam's joy, they went upstairs.

"Fuck knows what she's done but now's our chance," Dolly said.

They ran through the door that Steve had only just used. Liam could still smell his cheap aftershave lingering in the air. Typical they would hero worship all the worst parts of Deano.

As they quietly slipped down the stairs, Liam looked up. Figures were above them and someone sounded in agony. Once on the ground floor, Dolly stopped them in the stairwell. Martha had said they had three positioned on the exit.

"Can we fight them?" Claire asked.

"They'll be carrying," Liam replied.

Jonny didn't usually believe in firearms, but he would have broken them out for this. Liam could imagine how enraged he would be that they were beating him. Jonny didn't do losing. If anyone got remotely close to it, he just eliminated them. Job done.

They had managed to trap themselves and couldn't stay where they were for long.

"We storm them," Marco said, grimly. "There are three guys who aren't expecting it and four of us. Don't stop until we get to the car. Not for anything."

"I'll go first," Dolly said. "They don't know me."

"Then me," Claire said.

They nodded and Marco kissed Liam. "You last. They know you best."

With one last look of determination, Dolly pushed open the door and they bundled out. A lack of weapons hindered them, but Dolly had her housekeys between her fingers and Claire held her bag in front of her.

Sure enough, three lads were at the door. The first one didn't see it coming as Dolly smashed the keys into the side of his head. He let out an almighty yell and dropped to the ground clutching his hair, blood running through his fingers.

Claire dashed past them and just as the second lad raised a knife, she rammed into him. Her bag protected her from his attack, and she slammed the lad against the wall. It knocked the wind out of him.

The confusion gave Marco the chance to grab the third and kick his legs. Marco's strength was too much for the teenager, who hit the ground with an almighty thud. Dolly didn't wait for them to get up as she wrenched the front door open.

Liam made for freedom but suddenly his legs went from under him, and he rolled across the hard tiled floor, his body jarring at the shock of falling.

As he got his bearings, he could see Dolly and Claire had got through the door, but Marco stopped. He froze when he saw Liam on the floor. The weight of another body on his back made Liam struggle for breath.

"Run, for fuck's sake," Liam shouted.

Claire dragged Marco away as hands gripped the back of Liam's hoodie. The stench of cheap aftershave filled his nostrils.

"Where do you think you're going? I haven't seen you in ages, Li. How about we spend a bit of time catching up?"

Deano. Where the hell had he been?

Liam tried to struggle, but Deano had his arms painfully pinned to the floor with his knees.

"Oi, you. Get up, soft lad," Deano shouted to the nearest guy who had blood pouring from his temple where Dolly had hit him.

He staggered up.

"Tell the boss I've got the little traitor," Deano gleefully shouted at him.

It sickened Liam that Deano had been waiting for this moment ever since he joined the gang, and Liam had served him it on a plate.

The lad nodded and, still clutching the wound, he went up the stairs.

"I always knew there was something wrong about you," Deano said. "This is going to be so much fun."

He ground Liam's face into the tiles. Liam would not beg. Deano was still just a sentry. That was all he would ever be.

After what seemed like an age but was probably only minutes, the lift pinged and out walked Jonny, Harry, Aleck and Steve.

"Get him up," Jonny ordered.

Deano hauled Liam to his feet.

"You took some finding." Jonny sneered. "I might have known that old slag would have had you nice and safe." He slapped Liam hard across the face. "But once a tart always a tart, eh? Couldn't resist a bit of easy money," he said. "Is your new boyfriend paying her? She'll do anything for money, so they say."

Aleck and Steve sniggered.

"So Harry here tells me you've been fucking our Italian friend."

Liam stared at Harry who had the decency to look away.

"Did you think he would keep your little secret?" Jonny laughed. "Not a chance, poof. Harry is loyal. Your lot are cock mad — we knew you'd lead us to him. But you've cost me a pretty penny to do it. Randolph owed me a favour I wanted to cash in for planning permission for a new pool."

"My heart bleeds for you," Liam said, making sure his spit flecked on Jonny's face.

Jonny stood back, taking a handkerchief from his pocket and wiping his face. "It won't just be your heart bleeding soon. Get him upstairs. Might as well frame that old slapper for it."

"You can't let them do this," Liam said to Harry.

"What the fuck is he going to do?" Jonny continued, clearly enjoying himself. "Face it, kid, he sold you right down the river. Come on, let's get moving. I'm taking Sadie out for dinner tonight and you know how she gets if we're late."

They dragged Liam into the lift. It was a waste of energy to struggle. He just focused on the fact that Marco, Claire and Dolly had got away. No matter what happened to him, he hoped with all his heart that Marco would bring this bastard down.

He only wished he could have been a part of it.

Chapter Fifteen

They dragged Liam across Dolly's landing and into her lounge. It was unrecognisable from the little community space they had created these past few days. Her beautiful floral sofa had been slashed all over. The chair that she liked to sit in to knit and stare out of the window lay smashed to pieces on the floor. Even the pan Marco had cooked their lunch in had been emptied over the rug. The lads had left nothing sacred.

"You fucking bastards," Liam cried out. Rage flooded his system. If he could get his hands on them, he would rip them apart.

Deano and Aleck threw him down onto the sofa. A cloud of stuffing erupted around him, sticking to his face as the tears flowed.

"Aw he's crying," Deano announced. "I think we've touched a nerve."

Liam leapt up to attack him, but Deano pulled out a knife. "Steady on there, gay boy. Don't give me an excuse."

Jonny strolled into the room, closely followed by Harry. "Now then lads. Are we falling out?" Jonny said, rubbing his hands together. He examined the room as though he were in a slum. "The biggest tart in Manchester lives in this shithole. You learn something every day, eh?"

"She's worth a thousand of you," Liam muttered.

He'd been terrified of Jonny all his life, but today he couldn't have cared less. He had stopped caring. He'd probably end his days in this room, so what else had he got to lose? It was strangely fitting because he'd had the best times of his life between these four walls too. Jonny could never take that from him, no matter what he did.

"That's as may be, son," Jonny said, crouching down. "But she'll be fish food before long. Like the other two in your merry little band. I've spent the best part of a week trying to track you bastards down. Do you know how much that has cost me in lost sales?"

Everything came down to money. Liam tried to zone out, focusing on a stain on the carpet, but Jonny was never the type to be ignored and slapped Liam hard across the top of his head, causing him to cry out.

"I said, do you?" Jonny snarled.

Liam raised his head and met Jonny square in the eye. "With no dealers and no girls, I'd say fuck all."

He knew the next blow was coming. The predictability of it made him laugh which earnt him a third.

"Come on then, boss. Let's finish him and get out of this dump," Deano said.

Jonny leapt up and slapped Deano across the face. "How many fucking times do I have to tell you to shut the fuck up? You dare to give me an order?"

Liam stared in triumph at Deano. If he thought he would outlive him by very long, he was grossly mistaken. He overstepped the mark with Jonny all the time, a deadly mistake that he would learn the hard way.

Jonny rubbed his hand as his attention fell on Liam once again. He had given Deano quite a slap. The outline could still be seen on his cheek. Deano had the good sense to stay stock-still, but resentment oozed from his every pore.

"He's right, though. I haven't got all night. So, I'll tell you what we're going to do." Jonny licked his lips. "You're going to tell me where that Italian fuck's stock is and that will go somewhere to paying me back. Then, in recognition of all the years of service you've given me, I'll put a bullet in your brain instead of letting Deano here have his fun. How does that sound?"

Liam considered it for a second. It was probably the best offer he was going to get all day, but if he had to die, he needed to know something.

He glanced over at Harry, who turned away.

"Counteroffer," he said slowly. "I'll tell you where Marco's stock is if you tell me where my mother is. Then Deano can do what he likes. I couldn't give a fuck."

Jonny threw his head back and laughed. "Is that why you've stayed all these years? Jesus Christ, this would be funny if it wasn't so tragic."

"Stop messing around, Jon," Harry interjected. "Let the lad go if he promises to never come back. He's been a good worker. You owe him that, surely?"

Confusion spread across Jonny's face. "You going soft, Harry? I sincerely hope not. Losing one long-termer is unfortunate, but to lose two would really piss me off."

The other lads looked from one to the other. Liam got it—Jonny and Harry never disagreed. It would be unsettling to everyone.

"Anyway," Jonny said, walking over to the window. "The boy wants a deal and I'll give it to him. Your mother, sunshine, is at the bottom of the Ship Canal."

The blood rushed to Liam's ears. If he hadn't been sitting down, his legs would have given way.

"Not gonna cry again, are you?" Aleck said with a snigger.

Jonny grabbed a photo frame of Dolly's from the windowsill and sent it sailing through the air, narrowly missing Aleck and smashing against the wall. "Shut the fuck up, yeah?" he said calmly.

Aleck nodded miserably.

Jonny sat down on the sofa arm, near to Liam. "See, about ten years ago, there was a ton of bad pills doing the rounds. Nothing we could do to work out which was which. People started buying from out of town and bringing them in. Not good for business. So, I took a risk. Bought a job lot at a knockdown price from a lab in Peterborough. Real good deal that, Harry, remember?"

Harry didn't answer. He looked as though he were about to throw up.

"I had to test them of course," Jonny continued. "Your mother was a right one for a freebie. She'd suck a man off for a pint. Well, it was easy to offer these up to her. But fuck me, they were the bad ones. She was foaming at the mouth in less than an hour."

Liam had heard enough. He launched himself at Jonny and sent him tumbling to the ground. Liam fell on top of him, raining blows down on his ugly face. Deano and Aleck dragged him off and threw him back against the sofa.

"You *bastard*," Liam screamed. "Your day is coming, Jonny fucking Wellingham. I'm only sorry I won't be here to watch you squirm."

Deano and Aleck had him held tight, but he craned his neck to Harry. His tears were falling freely now, he didn't care what anyone in this room thought of him. "Why didn't you tell me? How many fucking times did I talk to you about her, and you knew?"

"I never knew about that, Liam," Harry said. He glanced at Jonny before shaking his head. "Honestly I didn't."

Still rubbing his head where Liam had punched him, Jonny got to his feet, enraged. "Of course I didn't tell you, you soft bastard. You'd have talked me out of it. I didn't want a fuss. It wasn't worth getting the cops all over us for some cheap tart. We just dumped her in the canal. Job done."

Liam's head was spinning. Shaun would never know. If only he could have told him. But then, Liam would be another mystery in Shaun's life.

"Come on then," Jonny said. To Liam's joy, Jonny had a slight quiver in his voice. No lad had ever attacked Jonny Wellingham. If he'd rattled him, then good. "I kept up my end of the bargain. Where's his stash?"

"You can suck my dick," Liam spat.

Jonny punched him hard in the stomach, and Liam doubled over in pain. "Don't give me any of your gay shit. Tell me where it is, or I'll cut your dick off and post it to your bumboy lover."

Deano yanked Liam's arm up his back. He would break it given the slightest encouragement. The pain seared through him and he clenched his teeth. He didn't want to give Marco away, but he hoped that they would be moving the stuff at that moment. "It's in his van. In the car park under the Beetham Tower."

"Isn't that reasonable?" Jonny said. "But you've proven you can't be trusted. What a conundrum. I know — how about we take a boys' trip there? Then when we've got the van, I'll do you a favour. The last one I'll ever do for you."

Liam just stared hard at Jonny. He had grown tired of giving him the satisfaction of dragging it out.

"We'll take you to the exact spot we threw your old mother in. It can be the family reunion you've waited your whole pathetic little life for."

Chapter Sixteen

They dragged him out of Dolly's flat, slamming him against walls — Deano taking great delight in making it as painful as possible. As they waited for the lift, he shoved Liam roughly away. He fell into Harry who backed off.

"You're a bastard, Harry," Liam spat. "I hope you never forget my face."

Deano slapped him hard across it. Blood trickled down from Liam's nose and he wiped it away with the back of his hand.

"No talking, gay boy."

The lift came.

"Take him first," Jonny said, holding Harry back. "We'll follow."

In the lift, Liam looked at himself in the mirror. Was this the last time?

He had the beginnings of a black eye and blood smeared across his face. He didn't care, just wished they would get it over with. All he hoped now was that Marco had got to the van before they did.

Marco. The thought of his kind Italian man made Liam lose his nerve. They had just begun this adventure and he had felt sure it would take them somewhere special. Of course, Jonny Wellingham would ruin that.

"If that shit isn't in the van, I'm going to cut you up, piece by piece," Deano said in Liam's ear.

"Just as well it is then," Liam replied. "I'd hate for you to have any fun."

They reached the ground floor and Deano shoved him out of the lift.

"See this, Aleck?" Liam said. "One day it'll be you. Deano isn't all that loyal."

"Shut the fuck up," Deano said.

But Liam could see fear in Aleck's eyes. Turning on one of their own was a big deal. He hadn't been particularly close to Aleck, but they'd got on well. They'd even played each other online in PlayStation games. If the last thing Liam did was sow dissent in the ranks, then he would do it gladly. Anything to strike back at that bastard in front. He only wished he could take it all the way and finish him.

The summer breeze was welcome when they got outside. Being cooped up in Dolly's flat for nearly a week had been driving him a bit stir-crazy, no matter how nice the company.

A vision of Marco in bed at Dolly's popped into his mind but he pushed it straight out again. If he thought about him, he would lose his nerve. He had to stay in the moment.

Two black Toyota RAV4 SUVs stood in the street.

"New cars, Deano?" Liam muttered. "Don't know how you do it."

"Skill," Deano replied. "Nothing you'd know anything about, you useless twat."

The windows were blacked out but Jonny and Harry would be in one, and Liam would be put in the other. Jonny did everything in his power not to be incriminated. He had a pathological fear of prison after being banged up for a three-year stretch in his twenties. It was his main weakness. That and Sadie.

They bundled him in the back. Steve had already got in the passenger side, and Aleck climbed in after him. Deano got in the front and fired the engine up. He pressed the inbuilt computer and the speakers burst into life with the sound of a telephone ringing.

"Ready, boss?" Deano asked.

"Ready," Jonny replied.

They set off. Deano floored it as they went through the housing estate that nestled around the big tower blocks, and they lurched around the corner.

"Calm it down, Deano. For fuck's sake," Jonny shouted down the line. "You knock a kid over and we're fucked."

Liam caught Aleck's eye and shook his head. Aleck looked out of the window quickly.

The main road into the city centre was around the corner and up to a T-junction. Liam thought about making a run for it, but they would have the child locks on the doors. He had been in Aleck and Steve's place so many times that he knew every trick in the book. Karma could be a bitch. He wracked his brains for what to do.

Deano drove slightly slower towards the T-junction.

"What the fuck is that car doing?" he shouted.

Liam sat bolt upright. Claire's car had appeared from behind a newsagent's and was hurtling towards them at breakneck speed. To his joy, Liam could see Marco in the front seat. A new fire burst into flames inside him. Jonny Wellingham would not have the last word. No matter what he had to do, he would get out of this. Liam braced for impact but the car sailed past them. They all spun around in their seats in time to see it plough into Jonny's car.

"Jesus Christ," Deano gasped.

Jonny's bonnet had concertinaed and steam rose from it. But Claire's car had fared better and was already reversing. "Shit!" Deano shouted.

He stuck the car into first gear to get away. Liam saw his opportunity and dove between the two front seats. Ignoring hands on his T-shirt trying to stop him, he grabbed hold of the steering wheel and yanked it to the side. The car swerved, throwing them all around.

"What the fuck you doing, you nutter?" Deano screamed. He tried to get control of the car, but it was too late. The impact of hitting the wall knocked the breath out of Liam. All the airbags deployed, throwing Liam back into his seat, jarring his back. He screamed out in pain.

Dazed, Liam didn't know which way was up. Suddenly a dishevelled Claire appeared at the window. She had a cut on her forehead and a swollen lip. Regardless, she wrenched the door open, and Liam crawled over a disorientated Aleck. He tried to grab Liam's leg, but Liam kicked out and fell to the floor. The gravel smashed into his face, making him see stars.

"Fucking hell, Liam. Are you all right?" she said, helping him to his feet.

"Can we just get out of here?" he urged.

She nodded grimly and led him to her car. As he ran after her, he caught movement in the corner of his eye. Jonny and Jack were getting out of the car and they had guns in their hands. The world stopped when he realised he was in the direct line of fire.

"I'm getting really fucking sick of this," Liam said.

Then Marco reversed Claire's car and drove in between them all, giving Liam and Claire a brief moment of cover. Dolly had the door open.

"Get in, quickly," she shouted.

Claire dove onto the back seat and Liam scrambled into the passenger side just as the first shot rang out. It glanced off the roof, smashing the sunroof glass. Shards of glass rained down on them.

"Go, go, go," Liam shouted, ducking down out of the way.

With a screeching wheelspin, Marco found first gear but immediately stalled it, making them all lurch forward. Someone let off another round and it hit the wing of the car on Liam's side.

"Jesus fucking Christ," Marco screamed.

He managed to get the car into life again and floored it. They headed up towards the T-junction, out of harm's way. For now.

"Left or right?" Marco screamed.

"Left," Liam replied. He desperately tried to get his heartrate to return to normal. He absolutely could not go to pieces right now.

The car lurched onto the main road to the sound of horns blaring as they cut up a delivery van and a car.

"Is he behind?" Liam asked.

"I can't see him," Dolly shouted. "Just get us out of here. Bloody hell, my heart."

"Now which way?" Marco said. He was struggling to get the car into second gear. Marco obviously wasn't used to driving clapped out cars like Claire's.

"Stop the car," Liam ordered.

"Are you mad?" Dolly and Claire said in unison.

They were going past a car showroom.

"Quickly. I know this city far better than you," Liam said to Marco.

Marco nodded and swerved the car over.

"Oh fuck, oh fuck, oh fuck," Dolly wailed.

Marco leapt out and sprinted around to the passenger side as Liam scrambled over. As Marco got in, he frantically looked behind them.

"Fuck. He's coming."

Liam didn't even wait for him to shut the door. He floored the accelerator and they launched straight into the traffic.

Harry might be a decent driver, but Liam knew his way around a car and the streets of Manchester far better. Liam had been negotiating these roads since before it had been legal for him to drive. He could do it in his sleep. For the first time that day, he felt in control, and he would prove to everyone just what he could do.

Pulling the handbrake, he took the corner tight and hit the dual carriageway hard. He thanked his lucky stars that it wasn't commuter time. In this part of Manchester, they would be sitting ducks.

"Is he still on us?" Marco shouted.

"Yeah, the bastard," Claire said. "About three cars behind."

"Fuck," Marco replied.

"No bother," Liam said with a grin.

He didn't know if it was the adrenalin from narrowly escaping a watery grave, the shock of finding out about his mother or he that had started to enjoy himself, but he threw himself into driving, weaving that beat-up old car in between the traffic, determination flooding through his system.

Another tight left and they sped past Manchester's grim Victorian prison, Strangeways. Liam had plenty of mates in there. He wondered what they would think if they could see him being pursued by Jonny, right under their noses. That would the talk of the wing.

"Still on us," Claire shouted. She had turned her back now and was watching the rear windscreen with Dolly holding her for support.

Liam swerved right, narrowly missing a bus. Up here lay a residential area — lots of twists and turns to lose them in. He took every single one, then took another right and they found themselves on a road that led them into town.

"Think," Liam said. "We need an endpoint. What are we going to do?"

"We need people," Marco replied. "If he stops us on one of these streets, we're as good as dead."

"People," Dolly said. "Hotel. We'll stay in a hotel until your uncle sorts his fucking life out. They'll find it harder to get to us."

"Good idea. Which one?" Liam said. "We can't keep driving around until the bloody petrol runs out."

"The Midland," Dolly replied. "It's the poshest we have. Doormen and everything. Even Jonny Wellingham wouldn't dare do a hit in there."

The Midland was Manchester's flagship hotel and sat slap-bang in the middle of the city centre. This wasn't going to be easy, but it was doable. Plus, the thought of sharing a five-star bed with Marco that night instead of being dead appealed to Liam.

"Hang on then," Liam said. "And I hope your credit card is working, Marco."

Marco grinned at him. "It's always working. You are fucking amazing, Liam."

Even when they were running for their lives, that smile could make him go weak at the knees. But he needed to focus. "Stop doing that," he said with a wink.

"Fuck flirting," Claire shouted. "Get this bloody done."

They tore past the Manchester Arena, Liam speeding down the road towards the city centre. There would be police everywhere, so he cut the speed. It seemed to go against every instinct, but if they got stopped, they would have a hard time explaining recent events.

"He's gaining," Claire said.

Seemingly Harry didn't have the same worries about the police. Jonny probably had them covered. He had powerful connections in the city.

The Northern Quarter was a district in Manchester that had been the industrial heart. The roads were still narrow and like a rabbit warren. Liam weaved through the back alleys, lurching one minute left, then right.

The Midland wasn't far away now. Liam knew of a multistorey right in the centre. He glanced in the rear-view mirror and couldn't see the others.

He spun the car at a right angle, and they drove up the rampway. Liam found a bay right in the middle of the other cars. The gunshots to the front couldn't be seen by a casual person driving past.

"Right, we've got to move," Marco said.

They scrambled out of the car. Liam's legs were like jelly but he could do this. He had to.

"When we get onto the street, we just go for it." Liam said. "You up for it, Doll?"

"Don't you pull that old woman shit with me, young man," Dolly said, checking her laces.

Liam winked at her which she returned with a grumpy scowl.

"Take the stairs," Marco shouted, scanning the place.

The smell of urine and cigarette smoke assaulted them as they ran down the concrete staircases. Liam was listening out for voices above or below them but mercifully they got to the bottom unscathed.

"Wait," he said.

He slipped out of the door at the bottom and searched the crowded shopping street for any faces he recognised. The coast looked clear.

"Follow me," he shouted.

They ran down the long street as fast as they could without drawing attention to themselves. They could keep the sprinting for if they really needed to. Marco glanced back.

"They're there," he panted. "Over by the coffee shop."

Looks like we really need to.

"Don't look," Liam yelled.

They followed tram lines down to St Peter's Square. The place where this all began.

"Is this—" Marco started.

"Shut up," Liam panted.

They crossed the square as fast as their legs could carry them. Office workers taking a stroll stopped to stare at the four people who were running like they had been possessed. Especially Dolly, whose mac had fallen open, exposing the bright pink negligee she hadn't had a chance to change.

The Midland stood at the other side of the square. The iconic building of Manchester that offered safety and shelter spurred Liam on. He nearly got clipped by a black cab and fell into Marco, who righted him.

Dolly got to the door first. The doorman stood in her way. "I'm sorry, madam—"

"Fucking move," Claire gasped out. "Or I'll tell your wife you like a dildo up your arse."

The doorman's eyes widened in recognition and horror, and he dutifully stood aside to let them in. It seemed a step too far for him to actually open the door. The marble floored reception of The Midland was huge and reassuringly busy.

They stood, panting at the elaborate floral display. Liam spun round to see Jonny, Jack and Harry standing on the pavement. CCTV and more than twenty witnesses were their protection and Jonny knew it.

Liam allowed himself to feel their victory. "We fucking did it," he managed.

Marco flung his arms around him.

"We're fucked if they're fully booked," Claire said.

"Leave it to me," Dolly said. She rummaged in her pocket for her phone. After finding a number, she put the device to her ear. "Alain. Dolly. I'm in your reception. We need two rooms. Can you do it? Yes? Good lad. Now is good."

She put the phone in her pocket. "General manager trumps doorman," she said to Claire, nonchalance in her voice.

They all burst into laughter that rang through the cavernous lobby of one of the poshest hotels in Manchester.

Chapter Seventeen

The bubbles overflowed onto the sandstone floor. Marco held Liam tight as tears rolled down his cheeks and into the warm water. Liam couldn't bear not to feel those arms around him. They lay in the huge bath for ages, Marco just holding Liam and waiting for the storm to subside. Liam had no idea when he wouldn't feel so empty. So much had happened to him that he didn't know if he even had the strength to try to process it.

"Just let it out," Marco murmured.

Liam was. As soon as they'd got to the room, he'd dissolved into floods of tears and Marco had insisted on a bath to keep him calm. It was working. The sobs were less frequent now, but when Liam had tried to move, the panic had overwhelmed him, and Marco had sunk into the bath with him, filling it with more hot water.

"I always knew she was dead," Liam said eventually, his voice croaky from all the sobbing.

"Deep down. But hearing him tell me why... I fucking hate him."

The strength in Marco's arms, encircling him, made him feel calmer, and the wave of fury ebbed away.

"When my cousins get here, we will teach Jonny Wellingham a lesson," Marco said. A steely determination in his voice gave Liam shudders. "Don't you worry, Liam. We will do it for your mother."

"You know, for the last ten years, I've made up all sorts of dreams about her. I used to hope she'd met a man and found a decent life somewhere. Then when she made enough money she would come back for me," Liam said, sniffing. "All the time she was at the bottom of the canal."

"Will you tell your brother?"

The thought of Shaun made Liam want to run away as fast as he could. How would he tell him? He had no choice, obviously, but beginning that conversation would be the hardest thing he'd ever had to do.

"I'll have to. I haven't spoken to him for a bit. He hates me being involved in all this. We had a row. A year or so ago."

"Family is important. I would do anything for mine."

Liam shivered.

"You're cold," Marco said. "Come on. We will get out. Do you feel ready?"

At last, Liam did. "Thank you, Marco. Thank you so much."

Marco kissed the top of his head. "You are my man. Anything you need is now my responsibility."

They got out of the bath. Liam felt totally helpless and when Marco gently towel-dried his body, the tears started to fall once more. He flung his arms around Marco, needing that connection again.

"Hey now, there can't be many more tears left in your body," Marco soothed. He kissed his neck as Liam nuzzled into him.

It amazed Liam how close he and Marco had grown. They'd known each other such a short time but Marco had changed Liam's whole life. He looked Marco in the eyes. Marco smiled and they kissed. It was a soft, gentle kiss that radiated love. Liam needed to feel his hands all over his body. His cock hardened at the thought.

Breaking the kiss, he put his hands on Marco's face. "Make love to me, please."

Marco nodded. Liam needed the distraction from the world that only sex could bring. Marco led him through into the bedroom. Their bodies still damp from the bath, they lay down on the huge bed.

His arms wrapped tightly around Marco, Liam hungrily claimed another kiss. Marco rested his arm lightly on Liam's waist as Liam stroked Marco's biceps. He ran his finger up the curves of his muscle and over his shoulder.

"I was terrified today," Marco said. "That I'd lost you. Dolly and Claire dragged me to that car. They're surprisingly strong."

Liam chuckled at the indignation on Marco's face. There were times that day when he'd never expected to laugh again.

"I mean it though," Marco said, tracing his finger down Liam's cheek. "I won't lose you, Liam. I don't think I can."

Liam threw himself into Marco's arms, need overpowering him. They kissed, Liam pushing his tongue into Marco's mouth. The stress of the day needed to be channelled and only Marco could do that for him. They ran their hands over each other's bruised bodies, reaffirming their love. He pushed Marco onto his back and straddled him.

Not breaking the kiss, Liam held Marco's arms above his head, so their hands clasped on the pillow. The warmth of his body against Liam's sent waves of pleasure across him, their beating hearts separated only by bone and tissue.

The summer evening was getting darker, and they lay in the expanding shadows.

Marco stroked Liam's body, sending chills through him. His hand cupped the back of Liam's head, holding him still for their kiss, then he gently rolled him over.

Marco moved to the foot of the bed and spread Liam's legs. He knelt between them and slowly ran his finger up Liam's chest. His touch was so light Liam could barely feel it, but his body seemed to come alive, desperate for Marco's touch.

Marco lightly rubbed Liam's nipple. The cold air had made them stand on end. Marco swirled around the nub. Liam groaned. He went to lift his head but Marco stayed him.

"Relax," he whispered.

No one had ever been there for his enjoyment only. Liam rested his head back on the linen pillowcases as Marco lazily stroked across Liam's chest to his other nipple. He took it between his two fingers and rubbed it. The contact sent more waves of pleasure through Liam.

His cock was solid and leaking pre-cum, his whole body on high alert.

Marco slowly explored the sides of Liam's abs. He traced every contour as Liam squirmed. Watching the concentration on Marco's face as he pleasured every inch of Liam's body, Liam knew he had fallen in love.

Marco stroked his hip bones. God, he needed to feel his touch on his cock.

Marco traced the skin along Liam's waist, his palm lightly grazing the tip of Liam's cock, which made him cry out. Marco stopped and glanced up at Liam. "You like?"

Liam could only nod. The blood rushed through his body while he waited for Marco's next move.

Marco ran his nails along the insides of Liam's thighs. Liam was incredibly sensitive there but didn't want to break the spell by moving.

He did cry out when Marco ran them along his balls. His cock twitched as if desperately trying to capture Marco's attention, and when Liam spread his legs wider, Marco responded by tracing along the seam of skin down to Liam's hole. He licked the palm of his other hand and rubbed the head of Liam's cock. The touch was so intense that Liam arched his back. He whimpered. He was totally in Marco's control now.

Marco seemed to get off on the power he wielded. He encircled his palm around Liam's hard cock and squeezed. With his free hand, he cupped his balls gently, then slowly massaged Liam's cock. Liam bucked his hips, wanting more from him, but Marco kept it at a maddeningly slow pace.

Marco's hand slid over Liam's cock, the warmth of his grip forcing Liam's body to relax. "That feels so good," he murmured.

Marco caught his eye and licked his lips.

He tugged harder, encouraging Liam to place his feet on Marco's strong thighs. Marco's biceps flexed as he rubbed Liam, whose body had started to warn him that the moment of ecstasy was coming. He tensed, desperate for the release.

"Oh fuck, Marco," he panted.

Marco gripped his balls hard. Liam let his whole body go, giving in to the sensation. It gripped him, taking him away from even Marco for that split second. With a yell, he came hard in thick spurts that fell over Marco's fingers and onto Liam's body.

Marco leant down and licked Liam's spent cock clean.

Once satisfied, Marco lay down next to Liam, snaking his arm around his waist and pulling him closer.

"What about you?" Liam said, his eyes heavy lidded.

"Don't worry about me," Marco whispered in his ear. "Having you in my arms is the best feeling I could ever hope for."

"Thank you," Liam said, stroking Marco's arm. "I'm sorry that I gave you away."

"What do you mean?" Marco asked.

They needed to talk about what had happened that day. They couldn't rest until they were truly safe and this hotel room only provided that for the short-term.

"They made me tell them where your stock is," Liam said.

He was terrified that Marco would be angry with him. The cousins were flying over, so they wouldn't be bringing any merchandise with them like Marco had.

"You haven't got proper supply lines set up yet," Liam said, aware he had begun blabbering again. "And now Jonny will have your only stock. He'll take the dealers back. They need to watch themselves though. He'll make them pay for being disloyal."

Marco chuckled. "Don't worry about my stock."

Liam extricated himself from Marco's grasp. "But Jonny will have it. You can't have sorted out more stuff yet."

Marco shook his head. "I moved the van before I went to the drop-off. It's in a lock-up on the outskirts of town. That's why I had to leave with you. The concierge at the apartment put me onto a place that his friend runs."

Liam couldn't believe it. Marco hadn't mentioned this the whole time they were at Dolly's, but then he'd had no reason to. Then it dawned on him. "I would have been killed."

Marco frowned. "I would never have let that happen to you. Never."

"But if they'd got me away, I would be dead now."

The realisation hit Liam like a brick. He had no illusion that Jonny would have done that whether the stock had been there or not. But the rage Jonny would have unleashed if he'd thought Liam had tricked him would have made the whole experience far worse.

"He'll be furious," Liam said. "He wanted that stock."

"Of course he bloody did. He will have warned the big boys far and wide. I had a couple from Liverpool on the hook, but I can imagine what he's told them. Once my cousins arrive, we will have some muscle. That might get them to change their mind."

Liam sat up. He desperately wanted to go to sleep. His body cried out for rest. But he would never sleep soundly until they knew what they were doing. "What's your plan?"

Marco sat up too, the overstuffed pillows supporting them. He reached for Liam's hand and took it. "I'll hit the phone in a bit. I've a van load of stuff that needs offloading. Claire can get in touch with some of the girls and we'll restart the online ads. I want Jonny to know we're back in business. He can fuck off if he thinks I'm hiding anymore. He's asked for it."

Liam shuddered. Nothing seemed to stop Marco. It was exciting and scary but completely addictive.

"What do you want me to do?" he asked. He wanted to be a part of bringing Jonny down, but more importantly, he needed to be by Marco's side.

"Are you sure?" Marco replied. "It got pretty dark back there."

"He killed my mother. Jonny Wellingham has made this personal. We go in as hard as you like. He fucking deserves it."

Chapter Eighteen

"Pass me the toast, please," Claire said.

Liam handed it to her.

They had ordered a room service breakfast in Dolly and Claire's room. Even Jonny Wellingham wouldn't dare to storm the corridors trying to find them, but if they sat in plain sight in the restaurant, they were poking the bear somewhat. Liam couldn't stop thinking about the rage that Jonny would be feeling right now. But his thoughts also strayed to Harry. He'd seemed as astonished as Liam when he heard about his mother. In some strange way, that gave Liam comfort.

"Did you sleep, love?" Dolly asked, snapping him out of it.

He shook his head and caught a worried glance between Marco and Claire. They meant well, but everything had become suffocating.

"I might go for a swim in a bit. I'm sure they have a pool. I reckon they'll sell trunks," Liam said, cutting up a sausage and swirling it around the plate. His appetite had left him, but Marco had been nagging him to eat.

"I'll come with you," Claire said. "A swim sounds wonderful. Especially after all this stodge."

Liam dropped his fork on the plate with a clatter, making everyone jump. "I won't die on the way to the swimming pool, Claire."

"I didn't mean —" she started

Dolly picked up the bottle of champagne and refilled her glass. "Now then, children. We've had a rough time, but there's no sense in falling out amongst ourselves."

"Are we safe here?" Marco asked her. "I mean really safe?"

Dolly took a sip of her drink and considered his words. "I doubt Jonny has a way in, but I wouldn't put anything past that slimy twat. I'm meeting Alain in an hour. I'll make sure we're safe." She winked at them.

"I appreciate your efforts, Dolly," he said, raising his coffee cup to her.

A flash of rage swirled in Liam. They couldn't possibly understand his feelings right now, but the idea that business went on as usual made him sick to his stomach.

"Are you okay?" Claire asked.

He had never been able to hide anything from her.

"I don't know," Liam said. "Everything feels different."

She leant across and rubbed his arm. "You've had the shock of your life, Liam. Today we can chill out and you don't have to do anything. We can watch a movie or something."

He got up and strode over to the window. The room overlooked the Manchester Conference Centre. They had an event on, and people were flitting in and out, chatting to one another and enjoying the sunshine. Their lives so carefree and normal.

"We've just swapped one prison for another," he said quietly. "When are we going to be able to do something? I don't even have a change of undies. I had to wash them in the bloody sink."

When they'd abandoned the car, they had left their bags. Dolly still had on her negligee although she had a better class of bathrobe to go with it. To his amazement her hair was flawless and she'd applied a thin layer of makeup. Did she secrete eye liner about her person?

"Leave that to me," Marco said, joining him at the window. "I'll get the concierge to go shopping for us. What's the point in staying in a fancy hotel if we can't make full use of it?"

Liam knew he was being unreasonable and lashing out. "I'm sorry, guys. I just feel weird."

"How about you have some alone time in your room?" Dolly said. "Marco can stay and watch some crap daytime television with us. We're only across the hall."

Grateful, Liam nodded. "I think I need that." He turned to Marco. "You don't mind, do you?"

Marco stroked his face. "I want whatever you need, Liam. Like Dolly said, we're just over here. Go and get some sleep."

Liam kissed him and walked out of the room. Once inside the room he had shared with Marco, he stepped out of his tracksuit trousers and threw his hoodie onto the chair.

Over by the window, he squeezed his underwear and socks. They would be dry soon. The irony wasn't lost on him that they were staying in the poshest hotel in Manchester and he had been rinsing his clothes in the sink. This wasn't his world.

He sank down on the bed, wrapping the soft throw over him. His body felt like a solid weight, but his mind remained in overdrive.

The pain didn't come just from knowing his mother had gone but from the fact that Harry had stood by while they were about to kill him. He had lived with the man and treated him like an uncle. He couldn't believe that Harry would have let them go through with it. His words imploring Jonny to let Liam go came back. The day was absolutely vivid in his mind, the fear and fury not leaving him.

Pulling the throw tightly round him, he curled into a ball.

He didn't think he could trust anyone except for maybe Claire. Then he thought about Marco. His arms brought safety, but everything had been turned on its head since he'd come into Liam's life. Logic would tell him to run as fast as he could, but how could he? Nothing would stop him from seeing this through.

Mercifully, sleep came as Liam worked things over in his head and he slowly drifted off.

* * * *

The harsh ringtone cut through his dreams. For a second, Liam had no idea where he was, but then he remembered he was in a swanky hotel with not a penny to his name.

His phone rang on the nightstand. Sunlight still streamed through the windows, so he couldn't have slept for long. He glanced at the clock on the television.

It was nearly one in the afternoon. He'd had a few hours.

Rubbing his eyes, he picked up his phone and suddenly jolted wide awake. He pressed Answer. "Jonny."

"You double-crossing little fuck," Jonny snarled. His voice sent rage burning through Liam's body. "I'll admit it, you've shown more balls than I thought you would."

Liam didn't care what Jonny said now. Having stared death right in the face, it made him feel freer than ever before.

"What do you want?" he asked, proud he showed no fear in his voice. That would drive Jonny mad.

"I want that stock," Jonny said. "I know you can't get any more. I've spoken to Greg Brooks and Shola Rose. They aren't going to sell your little friend anything. He's fucked."

"And you expect him to just hand over his stock?" Liam asked, incredulously. "He's got drop-offs to do, Jon. The weekend is coming. You know how Manchester likes to party."

It was a stalemate. Jonny might have the supply lines tied up coming into the city, but Marco still had the dealers. They went with the money. Then once the muscle arrived, Brooks and Rose and whoever else would soon change their tune. Marco had Jonny cornered and he knew it.

"You think you've got this all sewn up, don't you? You always were thick as fuck." Jonny sneered. "I said to Harry this morning how you've been lucky, but you don't have the brains to keep it going."

Liam sighed. He had no patience for empty insults. "Is that all you wanted?"

"Like I said, I had a good chat with Harry this morning," Jonny continued. "Poor old thing. Your betrayal has really taken it out of him. He trusted you more than any of us."

If Jonny thought Liam was going to feel guilty, he had seriously lost it. "Pass on my apologies," he said. "I know how he feels about betrayal. Walking out to leave me to your idiots didn't exactly make me want to jump with joy."

"Did I tell you Brooks sent me twenty lads and Shola is sorting me out with some girls? Your mate has done me a favour. I'm scaling up. Things will soon be back to normal."

Liam would have to warn Marco. Jonny never could resist bragging.

"Good luck to you, Jon." He sighed. "Let's hope these ones do what you say. Deano obviously thinks he's better than you. I wouldn't trust that one as far as I could throw him."

"I treat my lads how they need to be treated. They know who has their best interests at heart. That's why I sent Harry off to the coast for a few days. He needs some rest."

Liam frowned. What was he getting at?

"I mean I know Blackpool is a shithole," Jonny said.

Liam's heart thudded.

"But the sea is the sea, isn't it? You never know who he might bump into when he's there."

Shaun. "Don't you fucking dare drag my brother into this," Liam raged.

"You've done that, you stupid little fuck," Jonny spat back. "You know very well I don't just give up. That's why I've ruled this city for the last twenty years.

Get me that stuff by this evening or your brother will burn to death in his bed."

The call was terminated.

Liam threw his clothes on and dashed out onto the landing. He bumped straight into a couple dressed in expensive suits.

"What the —" the man exclaimed.

"Get out of my fucking way," Liam barked.

He fell on the door, banging for all he was worth. Marco answered and Liam pushed past him into the room. The couple were still staring open-mouthed as Marco slammed the door shut.

"What the fuck is going on now?" he said.

Claire sat in the chair next to the window. She looked at Liam. "Liam? What is it?"

"Harry is in Blackpool," he stammered. "He's going to get our Shaun if we don't give them the stuff. Today."

"Wait, what?" Claire said. "How do you know?"

Liam could hardly get his breath. Claire had got up now and held on to his arms. Marco stood at the door, frozen to the spot.

"Jonny rang me," Liam managed. "He's sent Harry to Blackpool. He said he either gets the stuff tonight or they'll do something to Shaun. It's not fair. He doesn't want anything to do with this."

Claire looked up at Marco. "Aren't you going to say anything?"

Marco crossed the room and sat on the end of the bed.

"We have to tell them where it is," Liam said.

Holding his phone up as some form of evidence, Marco shook his head. "I can't. He's closed the supply lines into the city. I've been messaging the dealers while you've been asleep. They're all ready for drop-offs tonight. I said outside this place. I don't care if they know who I am now."

Liam couldn't believe his ears. "You can't. They'll hurt my brother."

"He's bluffing. Most of his lads are out searching for us if we step foot out of here. One of the dealers told me," Marco replied.

Claire rubbed his shoulder, her touch the only thing grounding him and stopping him from attacking Marco right now. How could he be like this?

"You don't know that Jonny is bluffing, Marco. It's too big a risk," she said.

"And if I believe him and hand over everything? We're back to square one, but the dealers think I'm no match for Jonny," Marco reasoned. "When Enzo and Giovanni get here, we can show the supply lines from Liverpool and Hull that we have muscle. They'll change their minds."

Liam put his hand over Claire's. "Can you give us a minute? The other bedroom is open."

Claire gave dead eyes to Marco but nodded to Liam and walked out of the room. Liam stayed rooted to the chair he had slumped in.

"Are you telling me that you'll risk my brother's life to stay on top with Jonny?" Liam said in a steady voice.

Marco got off the bed and crouched in front of Liam. He put his hands on Liam's legs. The touch that had always calmed him filled Liam with revulsion. "Liam, look at me. This is important. There's thousands of pounds worth of gear in that van. After everything that happened in Naples, I have to prove what I can do."

Suddenly Liam could see the future. It all seemed to clear. "The only way you're going to stop Jonny claiming this city is to kill him," he said.

Marco shrugged. "And?"

"Then your superhero uncle comes with all the Italian muscle. Do you think it's over?"

"What do you mean?" Marco asked.

"Someone else will make a run for the city. Harry? Deano? Someone new? It will never end." Liam felt fatigue in his bones. "I've done this for ten years now. I'm tired of it. I'm tired of being around people who think profit is worth more than life."

Marco looked genuinely terrified. "Then we'll carry on until Uncle Z gets here, then we can do what we want. I just want to be able to hand over a business that is started. Surely you understand that?"

Liam pushed Marco's hands off his legs. "And you think we can build a life together if I blame you for my brother's death? I only found out about Mum yesterday."

"I can't do it, Liam."

Liam got up and strode over to the door.

"Where are you going?" Marco asked.

"Looks like Blackpool. I'm sorry, Marco, but I can't be around this anymore," Liam said, sadly. "You're no better than him. Just in a better package. I'll see you around, Marco. I'm done."

Chapter Nineteen

The seafront was heaving. Had every family in the northwest of England come out for the day?

"Still nothing?" Claire said.

They were bumper to bumper in traffic. Liam checked his phone for possibly the thousandth time. They had tried ringing Shaun, but it had always gone onto voicemail. "Nothing."

Liam worried like crazy that they couldn't get through, but also that Marco hadn't even bothered to ring him. After he'd left the room, Claire had gone in to get her things. Marco had still been in the chair.

She had tried to get him to change his mind, but he'd refused.

"*I told you,*" she'd said. "*This is our chance now to just go. We'll get Shaun and disappear. When Dolly gets my note, she can either ring us or do her own thing. It's over. Leave them to battle it out between them.*"

But the thought of it being over with Marco brought tears to his eyes. "I thought he saw me for who I am," Liam said, miserably.

Claire reached out and squeezed his leg. "He did. But you know the game. People get as addicted to it as their customers do to the shit they push on the streets. We've nearly died this bloody week, Li. We need to do the right thing for us."

At last, they were at the junction for the bed and breakfast that Shaun managed.

"Up here, second left." Liam had been here a few times. In the rare times that Jonny took a holiday, he would come and stay with Shaun. He hated Blackpool but they would always have fun doing something.

The Banyan Bed and Breakfast stood in the middle of a little side street. When Shaun and his ex had opened a yoga-themed guest house, Liam had been sceptical. He'd had egg on his face though, as it had proven to be a profitable niche. It seemed that a lot of people needed to find their zen before filling it with chips and rollercoasters.

They managed to park outside. The sign said *No Vacancies*, yet everything seemed abandoned. Where were the guests? He got out of the car and took in the building. Shaun had done a good job with it. Plants were flourishing outside, and it certainly looked like the nicest property on the street. Its neighbours had paint peeling and empty bottles in the gardens. But the eerie silence rattled him.

Claire was about to march up the path when Liam put out his hand to stop her. "Wait a minute."

"What?"

"All the other properties have vacancies and Shaun isn't answering. Harry is here already. Do we just go and knock on?"

Claire hesitated, looking up and down the street. Not a soul could be seen.

"If Harry is alone, he might panic if we both go in," Liam said, deep in thought. "Let me go. You stay out here."

"Are you sure?" Claire said.

Liam nodded.

With butterflies churning, he walked around the side of the property. If Harry had Shaun, they would be in his room at the back of the guest house. He snuck around the high brick wall and tried to peer inside. Shaun and another figure were sitting at the kitchen table. They were talking.

Marco's words echoed around in Liam's mind. What if Jonny had been bluffing? If Liam went in all guns blazing and Shaun had a new boyfriend around, he would look pretty foolish. But then he didn't care as long as his brother was safe.

While he dithered in what to do, the figure moved so the sunlight lit him up. It was Harry. Liam held on to the wall for support. His worst fears had been realised. Jonny had been deadly serious.

For a brief second, Liam studied the face that he knew so well. The face that had comforted him when Shaun had left Manchester. The face that had defended him when Jonny had got too nasty. The face that had left him to die only the day before.

Anger replaced fear and he let it power him to the glass kitchen door. Shaun saw him first and his eyes widened. Harry whirled around and they came face to face.

"You got the wrong Moseley brother, Harry. I'm here now," Liam said through the kitchen door.

Harry tipped his head and Shaun dashed to the door. He unlocked it and flung it open.

"Liam," he said, throwing his arms around him. "What the fuck is going on?"

"Get inside, both of you," Harry said.

He patted Liam down and took his phone. To Liam's dismay he had a gun, which he trained on both of them.

"Sit up that end. Hands where I can see them," Harry continued.

Liam and Shaun sat shakily at one end of the rickety old table. Harry lowered himself onto the chair he'd just vacated.

"What the fuck are you doing here, kid?" Harry asked.

"Don't 'kid' me," Liam spat back. "I'd be dead if it were down to you."

"What the fuck did you expect me to do? You were winding Jonny up and you know what that means. He wouldn't have killed you. I could have persuaded him to let you do a runner."

"Of course, you were just about to do that when you left me to them."

"It's true. I said we could use you as bait for that lad, whoever he is. Jonny as good as said if you would do that for him, he would have let you go. Then your little friend smashes into us and all hell breaks loose."

Liam didn't know whether to believe it or not. He desperately wanted to think that Harry would have his best interests at heart, but no one could be trusted. "Either way. I'm here now and not going to lead you to Marco or his shit, so you can fuck off."

Harry shook his head. "Jonny tells me what to do. You know that."

"How old are you?" Shaun said. "Forty-two, forty-three? Still taking orders from that piece of shit. Pathetic."

Harry picked up a glass and threw it at the wall, making them both jump.

"That's fucking right, and my orders are to kill you if we don't get that shit. The orders still stand no matter who else has joined the party."

"What the fuck do you expect me to do from here?" Liam said. "We've split. I can't do anything for you."

Harry looked like he had no idea what to do.

"Just say you did it. Finished him off and dumped the body. We'll disappear today and you'll never hear from us again," Liam said, trying to reason with him.

"Hang on a minute—" Shaun started.

"Shut the fuck up," Harry said. "I'm trying to think."

The tiny kitchen had begun to get claustrophobic. The heat from the day outside was making Liam sweat and he glanced at Shaun, who glared at him.

"You could come with us," Liam said to Harry. "This is your chance too."

Harry smiled. "Even after what I've done to you, you're still that decent lad deep down. The only way I can leave Jonny Wellingham is the day after his funeral. I know everything about him. He'd put such a price on my head, I wouldn't be safe on the fucking moon."

Liam could sense Harry wavering on what to do. "Then you'd better hope Marco's uncle is what he says he is."

Harry frowned. "Uncle?"

Liam realised he had said too much. "Forget it."

Raising the gun, Harry's face suggested he was going to do anything but that. "You'd better start talking."

Liam glanced at Shaun.

"Who the hell is this Marco?" Shaun asked. "And why has he brought trouble to my bloody door?"

"Marco is an up-and-coming gangster who Liam here has been screwing," Harry said, still pointing the gun at them. "But it seems he's not the chancer that Jonny thinks he is. Speak, Liam."

Miserably, Liam shrugged. "Okay, fine. His uncle is a bigshot in Italy. He wanted Marco to come here and sound everything out. Marco got a bit carried away though. His uncle is pissed off and sending more muscle. This is not over yet, Harry."

"Who is his uncle?"

"I don't know," Liam said. "He just called him Uncle Z."

"Uncle Z? Doesn't mean fuck all," Harry said.

They were stuck now. Liam could see Harry's dilemma. He couldn't get any further information out of Liam, but Jonny would kill him if he returned with nothing.

"Let Shaun go at least," Liam said, eventually. "He can't help you."

Harry seemed lost in thought. Liam smiled at Shaun. He wanted to reassure him, but Shaun didn't appear to be swayed.

"This is going to be a war, isn't it?" Harry said, quietly.

Liam nodded. "Now Jonny has Greg Brooks' lads, Marco will match him, and they will tear the city to pieces."

To Liam's astonishment, Harry began to laugh.

"What's so funny?" Liam asked.

Harry stood. "I owe you, Liam. I should never have risked your life like that. Come with me. We're going to finish this."

Shaun grabbed hold of Liam's arm. "No. Leave him alone."

Harry still had an amused expression on his face. "Nothing like that, Shaun. Honest. We're just going for a walk along the seafront. Come on, lad. You can trust me."

Liam had a gut feeling that he could. Something in Harry's voice made him realise he should go. "Claire's outside," he said to Shaun. "Let her in and I'll be along in a bit."

"I might have bloody known she'd be here," Harry said. "She's a decent friend to you."

"Unlike you," Liam replied.

Harry nodded and opened the door. They walked down the back alley and onto the next street that led to the packed promenade.

"You're an idiot," Liam said. "What's to stop me running?"

"Nothing," Harry said, pocketing the gun. "Except you're as curious as me."

They walked in silence until they were on the busy seafront. Music played from amusement arcades and children begged for more money to spend unwisely.

They crossed the still stationary traffic and found a bench to sit on that looked out onto the dirty Irish sea.

"Now you've got me, what's the big revelation?" Liam asked.

Harry kicked a pebble with the side of his foot. "What I'm about to tell you, you can use or not. But if Jonny is finished, it gives us both the chance to get out. I know I have no right to ask you anything, Liam, but I want you to think about it."

Liam couldn't believe that Harry had the cheek to ask for his help, but Harry knew him better than most people. His take that Liam would be curious had been spot on. "Go on."

"Jonny is bluffing about Greg Brooks. He's in deep shit with him and Shola. He owes them thousands and with sales stopped, they're after his bollocks."

Liam's mind was racing. Jonny had been bluffing, but not in the way that Marco thought. He needed this stock desperately.

"Actual fact, Wellingham's Boys are pretty fucked all round. When I got here, Jonny rang me to say Aleck and Jack are missing."

That only left Deano and Steve in his inner circle. Jonny always had other muscle but not ones that knew the way his mind worked. Liam's first instinct was to tell Marco, but he would not get involved any further. Especially not with someone who thought his brother's life so dispensable.

"What are you going to do?" Liam asked.

"Tell Jonny what's happened of course," Harry said. "I'll say you turned up, fought and got the gun. I barely escaped with my life. What you do with the information is your business."

Even though the betrayal still burned, Liam felt pity for Harry. "I've left Marco," he said. "I just want out of this."

Harry nodded sadly. "I don't blame you, kid. I'll cover you. I promise. There's no getting out for me. I should have known, really."

Liam sighed and got up from the bench. "Take the scenic route home, yeah? I'll see what I can do."

Harry held his hand out for Liam. "This is goodbye then?"

Liam took the hand and shook it. "Goodbye." He set off to The Banyan. He could give Marco one last phone call. That was when he realised that Harry had his phone. But when he looked back, Harry had gone.

Liam scanned up and down the seafront but couldn't see him.

Maybe he should just accept it as a sign that things were over. If he couldn't get in touch with Marco, all that he had left was to run for a bit. Persuading Shaun to do that would be another matter.

Walking up the back alley, he thanked everything that he had Claire with him. If he couldn't persuade Shaun to take a holiday, she certainly would. He let himself in the kitchen door, but the room was empty. There were voices coming from the front parlour that Shaun used to serve breakfast in. Throwing his coat down on the chair, he made his way through.

"He's a proper little detective. I'd have got us all shot up by barging through the front door," Claire said.

Liam pushed the door.

"Oh, your brother has many surprises up his sleeve," came a female voice.

It couldn't be, could it?

Pushing the door open, he saw Claire and Shaun sitting on chairs, but on the sofa sat Dolly and a man he'd never seen before.

"Dolly," Liam exclaimed. "What are you doing here?"

"She brought me."

Liam whirled around and by the window stood Marco.

Chapter Twenty

How had it all happened? His first instinct was to run to Marco but then he remembered how Marco had reacted when his brother's life had been on the line. Frozen to the spot, he just stared at him.

Marco looked so hopeful it made Liam's heart want to break. The world felt as though it had been spinning out of control for days now. He'd thought talking Harry round would have made it stop, but now the cause of the chaos sat in his brother's lounge.

He couldn't focus and wanted to know what had been said while he had been out with Harry. Then his gaze fell on Shaun. He had so much to tell him. The rest of the room would have to wait. "Can we go and talk?" Liam asked his brother.

Shaun nodded. "I think we'd better."

His face suggested to Liam this would be harder than he'd even expected.

"Liam—" Marco started.

"Leave them," Claire interrupted. "We'll be waiting."

She nodded at Liam as Shaun crossed the room and led him out. Liam gave Marco one last look. Deep down, he really did hope he would wait.

Shaun gestured upstairs and Liam followed him. It took him right back to a time not long after their mother had left, and Liam had been found to be truanting from school again. He had received a stern telling off that afternoon, but today he genuinely feared Shaun's words.

They walked through Shaun's bedroom and onto an outside terrace. The view wasn't much, just the roofs of other guest houses, but Shaun had a bistro table and plants.

"Welcome to my paradise," he said.

Liam sat and Shaun followed suit.

"Shaun, I—"

But Shaun held his hand up. "Let me set the ground rules first," he said firmly. "I need to know. Am I still in danger?"

Unable to lie, Liam nodded miserably.

"For fuck's sake," Shaun said. "I might have known you would drag me into this one day. Didn't I always say that hanging out with that greasy bald shite would end up in trouble for us all? I think you'll find I did."

"Can I speak now?" Liam asked.

"Fine, go on. I've heard a bit of it from Claire and whoever the fuck else has invaded my bloody business. Who is the handsome one? Tell me that first. Is that the one Harry said you were banging? Not bad, brother."

Liam sighed. "I met him a week or so ago. But listen, Shaun—"

"Ah, you've told the world you're gay now? About time."

Liam was a little taken aback. He had always been honest with Shaun, but Shaun lived his life way more openly than Liam and thought everyone should.

"I couldn't face it. Not when running with Jonny. You know what he's like."

Shaun looked annoyed. "Don't you realise that's why I wanted you out of there? Jonny Wellingham is a frigging dinosaur."

"I stayed because I thought Mum would come home," Liam mumbled. He couldn't put it off any longer.

"Mum —" Shaun began.

Liam put his hand on his thigh. "Wait. I have to say this. I thought Mum would come back and Jonny would hear about it first. That's why I stayed. But that bastard thought he would finish me off yesterday and he taunted me with the truth."

Liam couldn't believe he had to do this. "She's dead, Shaun," he blurted out. "Jonny killed her. She didn't run off with some guy. He used her as a tester for what he thought were tainted goods."

They both stared at each other. Liam didn't know what else to say.

Eventually Shaun broke the silence. "I guess I always knew deep down, but it's hard to hear it, isn't it?"

He got up and stood at the balcony railing, staring over the rooftops and down to the sea in the distance. Liam joined him.

"I'm sorry I didn't listen to you," Liam said quietly.

"You never have done," Shaun replied. "You always know what's best. How's that working out for you?"

He couldn't even argue this. He had never had any faith in Shaun but looking at the little business he'd built, he had to ask himself whether he had been right. Yes, he had a decent amount of cash in the bank but at what cost? He daren't even go to the shops to spend it.

"I don't know what's best right now," Liam said, quietly. "I haven't got a fucking clue."

"Are we back to sexy arse downstairs?" Shaun asked. "You've just told me my mother is dead and you want to talk about your love life?"

"Not just that." Liam sighed. "We're not safe. We might need them."

Shaun sat back. "And you're just thrown into the arms of your protector?"

"No chance," Liam said. "I don't trust him anymore. I honestly thought he was different. But he didn't mind leaving you to Harry if it meant getting one over on Jonny."

Shaun frowned. "Yet he's in my front parlour. Why do you suppose that is?"

Why had Marco come here? Liam had been so focused on telling Shaun everything he'd pushed that out of his mind. "What did he say?"

"He should probably tell you that," Shaun said. "But take it from me — nothing is as it seems at the moment. Claire told me I should pack a bag. Is that your advice?"

Liam felt as though he'd hit a wall and had no idea what the future could possibly hold. Then he remembered what Harry had told him. "There's a chance I can finish this. You should come with us for now, but once Jonny is down, you'll be safe again."

Shaun nodded. "I had better be, Liam. I didn't ask for any of this. Fuck's sake."

He went into his bedroom and got an overnight bag down from the top of the wardrobe. Liam watched through the window. It had been over a year since he'd seen Shaun, but his brother looked well. Even though they had a lot of shit to deal with, Liam loved him. It made him feel better just having him around.

"Are you going to sort it or not?" Shaun said as Liam was transfixed to the spot. "I mean it, Liam. I will come with you now but I don't intend on a major life change, thank you. You might want to run around thinking you're Tony bloody Soprano but some of us are content with a quieter life."

Liam sighed and walked through the room to the door. "I really am sorry, Shaun."

"Don't be sorry," Shaun muttered. "Be busy fixing it."

Liam went to go but Shaun took hold of him and they hugged. It was the most powerful, strength-inducing hug that Liam had had. He clung to his brother.

"She'll be pissing herself watching us giving Wellingham the run around," Shaun said as they stood back.

Staring into Shaun's eyes and knowing their mother had gone, Liam shed a tear. So did Shaun.

"Now off you go," Shaun said.

Without answering, Liam went down the stairs and into the front parlour. Only Claire and Marco were waiting.

"Where's Dolly and that guy?" he asked.

"Gone for some food. Turns out Alain knows a half-decent restaurant. In Blackpool of all places," Claire replied.

Liam sat on the sofa. Marco never took his eyes off him. He didn't seem to have moved since Liam went upstairs.

The front parlour had been decorated in calming tones. Shaun held yoga classes in here when the weather was horrible. Hot summer days he took his guests onto the beach.

No matter how much chanting had been done in this room, Liam doubted he would be able to keep calm. So many conflicting emotions were swirling around in him. He wished he knew which one to trust.

"How did it feel coming face to face with the man whose life you were quite happy to throw away?" Liam said to Marco. He needed to keep that anger right where he could use it.

Marco crossed the room and sat next to him. Worry etched across his face, which made Liam want to fall into his arms. But he had to stay focused. The way out lay open to him, Shaun and Claire. He couldn't let his lust for Marco ruin it.

"Can I speak?" Marco said.

"Shall I disappear?" Claire asked.

"No," Liam said. "I can't be trusted around this fool. Stay where you are."

Claire nodded and glanced from Liam to Marco.

"I realised pretty much as soon as you'd gone how fucking unreasonable I was being," Marco began. "I know that doesn't excuse me for staying in the first place. Dolly persuaded Alain to bring us here. I don't want to know how."

Marco gave him a hopeful grin, that beautiful lopsided smile that went straight to Liam's legs. But today he sat upright and cleared his throat. He absolutely would not be charmed into submission.

"Well that all sounds like you're Mr Perfect again," he said, struggling to maintain the dead-eyed stare he was determined to exude. "What is it you need from me now? I figure there's something because you've left the shop unmanned. Not like you."

Marco glanced nervously at Claire before turning to Liam. "I don't need anything. I just wanted to make sure you were alive. I will go."

He started to get up.

"Wait," Liam said. "Sit down. If you can tone down the drama, I'll bring you up to speed."

Slowly Marco sat. "Go on. I'm all ears."

"Harry only spared us because I promised to give him the location of the stuff. You're going to give me it in the next five minutes and I'm going to do just that."

Marco held his hand up. "Now wait a minute—"

"No, you wait a minute," Liam barked. He had stunned Marco into silence. "My plan was to come back to Manchester and fuck it out of you, but you've saved me a job. Then I'd do a runner with Claire and Shaun. But Harry told me something that threw everything up in the air."

"What's that?" Claire asked.

"Jonny's bullshitting about his reinforcements."

"What?" Marco exclaimed.

"In fact, he's right in the shit with Gary Brooks and Shola Rose. He owes them a lot of money."

Marco stared at him, seemingly lost in thought. "That's why he wants my stuff. He needs to get trading as quickly as possible."

"Absolutely. Plus, Aleck and Jack are on the missing list. He's only got Deano, Harry and Steve," Liam continued. "It's an open goal for you. Problem for us is, no matter what Harry says, Jonny Wellingham won't rest until I'm six feet under. He doesn't take kindly to traitors."

"That's true," Claire said. "Where would we run to?"

Liam shook his head. He hadn't got that far. He didn't even have a passport. They would have to go a long way to evade the reach of Jonny Wellingham.

"Exactly, so when I was walking back to this place, I made up my mind that we'll finish him. If he's lost his contacts and his cash, he'll have more on his plate than worrying if Harry pissed his pants at having to put a bullet in me," Liam said.

Marco reached out to him. "Thank you."

But Liam pulled away. "Don't get any ideas that I'm doing this for you, you piece of shit. You're a means to an end. Once we've done my plan, we're through."

Marco looked as though he were about to burst into tears. "Liam–"

"I mean it," Liam said. "I'm getting out of this life once and for all. There's nothing you can say, so you may as well shut up and be grateful you've got our help."

Miserably, Marco nodded and sat on the sofa.

"Do you have a plan?" Claire asked.

"Yep," Liam said. "What's the point in Jonny trying to steal your stock if he's got nowhere to hide it? We're going to burn him to the fucking ground."

Chapter Twenty-One

"His gates are still fucked," Marco said.

"That'll work in our favour," Liam replied. "They can't trap us."

"There'll be cameras everywhere though," Claire said. "What are we going to do about them?"

They carried on driving past the entrance to Jonny's house. A couple of lads were supposedly guarding it, but they were too engrossed in something on their phones.

"Look at them," Marco muttered. "Just wait until he meets our men."

The ones that are taking their time to arrive, Liam thought to himself. There were a lot of promises coming out of Italy, but so far, no actual progress.

Claire parked up in a layby. Jonny's house sat on a tree-lined street in the middle of suburban Manchester. Hardly anyone could be seen. Only cleaners and gardeners moving to and fro while the rich owners were in some office making even more money.

"Shaun had better be all right," Liam said.

They had got back to Manchester in record time. No one would be expecting them but even so, Liam had hated leaving his brother.

"Dolly will keep an eye on him," Claire replied. "I think poor Alain is regretting getting mixed up in all this. Dolly must have some serious moves, that's all I can say."

"We ready?" Marco asked from the back seat. "Let's get this over with."

Liam got out his mobile and dialled Harry's number.

"You were supposed to get in touch yesterday. We had a deal," Harry said in answer.

"Took me all night to get the information out of him," Liam replied.

"I don't want to know," Harry muttered. "Well?"

Liam glanced at Marco. "It's in a lock-up near Strangeways. I'll text you the address."

"And where are you now?"

"We're still in Blackpool. I told him it was too dangerous to come back."

Liam was sure he could hear his heartbeat thudding almost out of his chest. The silence on the other end was excruciating as Harry digested this information. Liam had never been able to lie to Harry, but he hoped this time he would actually manage it.

"You'd better not be shitting me, Liam. If you are, I won't be able to protect you," Harry said, grimly.

"Because you did such a good job of that at Dolly's," Liam replied.

The line went dead.

"Well?" Marco asked.

"Now we wait," Liam said, sending the text message with the address on.

They sat in the car for what seemed like hours with no movement from Jonny's house. Claire had bought some sweets for the journey, so they all munched noisily through them.

"Imagine if we're under surveillance," Claire said. "Yes, your honour, we observed them absorbing far too much sugar."

"They are clearly highly trained criminals with a love of..." Marco held up a strange-looking sweet. "What the fuck is this?"

"That's a rhubarb and custard," Liam said with a smile. "The king of sweets. Try it."

Marco popped one in his mouth. Eventually his eyes lit up. "That is amazing."

Liam raised an eyebrow. "You're easily pleased. Just wait until you try a Kola Kube."

"I would like that," Marco said.

Liam's heart sank when he saw Marco's face. They had discussed the plan only since leaving Blackpool — Liam absolutely refused to speak about what had gone on between them. They were dead and buried. They had to be. He had absolutely convinced himself of that.

"What happens after today remains the same," he said, firmly.

Marco nodded. "Can't blame a boy for dreaming though."

Just as Liam started to reply, Claire straightened up. "We have movement. Get down."

They slumped in their seats. With the front end of her actual car still mangled, Marco had insisted they hire one in Blackpool. He had no respect for how Jonny operated, but even he would recognise a bashed-up car that he'd been in a chase with only days before.

The SUV had blacked-out windows, but Liam could make out Harry and another figure in there.

"Was that Steve?" he said, hardly daring to breathe.

"Could have been," Claire mused. "Although he's got a few new faces. Who are the lads on the gate?"

"Ugh. Kane Sanderson and Pete Bull," Liam replied. "They've been trying to get into Jonny's inner circle for years. Looks like there's a vacancy. He's desperate if he's using them. They're as thick as mince, honestly. But I guess they'll have to be if Deano's bossing them around."

They waited a few more minutes but no other vehicle came out of the driveway. Claire had logged into the CCTV app that covered the lock-up and they all stared at the phone they had propped up on the dash. They didn't want to strike only to find out that Harry had nipped to the shops for fags and would be back in minutes.

The city centre was about thirty minutes' drive from Jonny's house, so they settled in. It passed tediously slowly and just as Liam was about to suggest a game of I-Spy, movement in the corner of the screen caught their eye.

"What was that?" Marco said.

They all stared, absolutely transfixed. Sure enough, the door to the lock-up was being wrenched open from outside. The morning sunlight was already stealing through the gaps and lighting up the dusty floor of the old garage on the screen.

"Is that enough?" Marco said.

Liam nodded. "Yeah, I reckon. Claire, you keep watch in case it isn't them. But it's got to be. They won't take long to get that van going. You know they'll sell that shit no matter what happens?"

Marco shrugged, giving his handsome grin.

Liam narrowed his eyes. "There is product in there?"

"Only a little bit. I didn't want to...how you say...put all my eggs in the fox's basket."

Claire sniggered. Liam couldn't believe this. "You said it was all in a lock-up."

"It is. Just not all in the same place. Come on, Liam Moseley. You didn't expect me to give it all away, did you? I'm superstitious. This gear has to be sold by Marco Ponti."

"Fuck's sake," Liam said. "We need to move. They will go mental when they realise."

Claire fired the car into life, and they drove down to the end of the road.

"Just up here," Liam said.

They were in one of the little cul de sacs that surrounded the edge of the posher houses. Arthur Crabtree's house backed onto Jonny's garden. He'd been recruited to the cause a long time ago. Liam highly doubted Jonny would have had the time to tell Arthur that Liam had gone rogue.

Liam and Marco got out of the car. Liam turned to Claire. "Keep the engine running, yeah?"

She nodded. "For freedom."

He waved and joined Marco at the gate. Arthur kept his garden absolutely immaculate. Liam always worried that he messed it up just by walking down the path.

He knocked on the door and an elderly man opened it.

"Liam. Well, there's a sight for sore eyes. I haven't seen you in a while," Arthur said with a kindly expression. Liam often called for a brew at his place. He had a ton of fascinating stories to share.

"We need to get through, Mr Crabtree," Liam said. "Is now a good time?"

"Of course. Anything for you lads. You know that."

Arthur opened the door wider. Liam and Marco went in. At the doorway, he gave a last look back at Claire. She stuck her thumb up before reversing the car and driving out of the little road.

Things were afoot. He had to see this through now. It was the only way that he, Shaun and Claire had any chance of starting a new life, far away. He owed this to his brother.

Liam followed Marco through the beautifully kept house. A television blared in another room. Liam envied Arthur his simple life. His life had got so complicated he worried he would never get out of the spider's web he had found himself in.

Then he thought about Shaun, nervously waiting for them. He had to fight to get his freedom. If they did this right, Jonny Wellingham would never bother his family again.

They followed Arthur's little garden path to the shed at the end. Arthur undid the lock on the door and pulled it open. The hinges squeaked. It had been a while since they'd had to use this.

"Thanks, Mr Crabtree."

Arthur put his bony hand on Liam's arm. "Go steady, son. Whatever you're up to. Go steady."

He hardly dared look at Marco. Did Mr Crabtree know they were double-crossing Jonny?

"Nothing major happening today, Mr Crabtree," Liam said with forced cheerfulness. "Just moving a bit of stuff. That's all." He patted Marco's backpack.

Arthur stared hard at both of them before shaking his head. "You kids." He chuckled to himself as he walked up the path towards his house.

"I thought he had rumbled us then," Marco whispered.

"Yeah, me too," Liam replied, watching Mr Crabtree go inside. "We can't fuck about."

"How come Jonny has that old duffer on the payroll?" Marco asked.

Something about the way he said it annoyed Liam. "Arthur was the best forger in Manchester. He made a bloody fortune. He likes to keep his hand in."

Marco glanced back at the house. "You never can tell about people."

Liam led the way into the shed. It had been kept empty save for an old lawnmower and some cobweb-covered plant pots. On the other side, was a second door.

Slowly, Liam forced the door and it opened up to Jonny's garden. They used this rat run when Jonny didn't want stock bringing through his front gates. The police regularly set up camp there.

They stole out of the shed and crouched down in the trees at the foot of the garden. They were near to the tennis court and Jonny's pool house lay in the distance.

"He only has cameras on the gate and the front door. The last thing he wants is a record of what goes on in the rest of this place," Liam told Marco.

"People could still be watching from the windows," Marco replied.

It seemed like such a small stretch of ground, but it might as well have been miles.

"Get down," Marco urged as a young lad came around the side of the pool house. The trees gave plenty of cover but if someone really looked, they would see them.

Liam didn't recognise him. He didn't seem to be more than twenty. Jonny must be grasping at straws for muscle if he had to bring in kids like this.

The lad produced a cigarette from his pocket and lit up.

"For fuck's sake," Marco muttered. "We haven't got time for this."

"Tough shit. We show ourselves and he'll sound the alarm," Liam whispered.

They crouched and watched him, willing him to hurry up with his smoke. All noises seemed heightened to Liam.

"I don't want you to go," Marco whispered.

"What?" Liam replied, unable to believe Marco's sense of timing.

"I said, I don't want you to go," Marco repeated.

Liam stared at him. "I heard you. I'm just amazed that this is the time you choose to speak about our relationship."

Marco winked at him. "We're in a relationship then?"

"Fuck off, Marco."

"Seriously, Liam. We could get killed doing this and I want to tell you something."

Watching the young lad taking his time on his cigarette, Liam wished he would stub it out immediately. Marco clearly had a melodramatic speech incoming and Liam needed to stay focused.

"Whatever it is, can you save it until we're done here?" Liam asked. "I promise I'll come and speak to you the first chance I get. Now is not the time, Marco."

"Fine. Have it your way. But just in case, I love you, Liam Moseley. Not lust, not like, but love, and there's nothing you can do about it."

Liam glanced at him. The triumph on his face that he had got this out made Liam's heart melt. If they had been anywhere else in the world, he would have kissed Marco and let the worries of the last few days dissolve away. But they were in Jonny Wellingham's garden waiting to strike a fatal blow to his business and the one obstacle had just stubbed his cigarette out and headed around the building.

"Time to move," Liam said. He got up from their covered spot. "We can discuss this at a later date, and before you make assumptions, that is not acceptance."

Marco nodded dejectedly. He pointed at the side door and made sure the backpack was secured on his back.

Liam and Marco dashed across the lawn. Liam expected shouts or an alarm to be raised at any second. They were on open ground, but to his amazement they got to the wall of the pool house with no commotion.

Catching his breath, Liam pointed over Marco's shoulder. Marco crept along the side of the wall and carefully poked his head around the corner.

He gestured the all-clear to Liam. With nerves that threatened to overpower his whole body, Liam followed Marco around the corner. For a split second, they would be in full view of the house, but it was done in the blink of an eye.

"Fucking hell," Marco said, once they were in the snooker room.

"Be quiet," Liam ordered. He checked the bathroom, kitchen and dorm. "All clear. Come on upstairs."

"I think I remember the way," Marco muttered.

They made it up to the storeroom where they had held Marco. It felt awful to be in here again. The gear was still piled up in crates and the chair where they had held Marco still lay on the floor, abandoned. Liam had half expected Jonny to get nervy and move the stock, but he wouldn't have a reason to if he thought his fortress was still protected.

Marco got out the bottles of barbecue lighter fluid they had bought at a petrol station on the way. It was crude, but they didn't have time to get anything more effective.

They set about emptying the bottles over the crates. Jonny would see millions go up in smoke once they got this going. This would finally be the ending they all craved, then they could see what the future held.

"Lighter?" Marco held his hand out.

"What the fuck do you think you're doing?"

They both whirled around to see Sadie standing in the doorway.

Chapter Twenty-Two

"Sadie," Liam said.

Where had she come from? He glanced at Marco who looked ready to finish her off. Once more, Liam couldn't trust his actions.

"You don't know what's going on," Liam said. "Just get out of here, honestly."

But Sadie didn't come across as though she had any intention of taking orders from Liam. She strolled into the attic. "It stinks in here."

Marco glanced nervously at Liam. They needed her out of here.

"Smells like betrayal, Liam," Sadie continued. "My dad has been telling me all about you two perverts. Imagine his surprise when he finds out you're in our attic."

"Don't worry about your slimy father. He's off stealing our stock," Marco said. "Fair's fair."

Sadie frowned. "My dad is in the kitchen next door chopping up things for lunch. What a good warm-up for him." She held up the panic alarm that Jonny insisted she always have. It was flashing.

"Fuck," Liam said.

Liam darted for the door, but Sadie got in his way. She clawed at his face, sending him staggering backwards. He fell to the floor and in a second, Sadie attacked him, once again gouging into his skin with her fake, dagger-sharp nails. Marco grabbed her by the waist and dragged her off Liam. She screamed with frustration, still lunging for him.

Marco slammed Sadie hard against the wall. Dazed, she fell to the floor. Liam scrambled to his feet.

"Run," Marco shouted.

They dashed down the stairs. To Liam's horror, Deano and Steve were at the French doors.

"Fuck!" Liam shouted.

Steve fell onto Marco, raining punches down on him. Deano forced his way past them, aiming straight for Liam. The hungry leer on his face told Liam he was clearly revved up for this opportunity after losing out at Dolly's.

Liam had never have been much of a fighter, but he readied himself. Everything he had suffered in the last couple of weeks had come to this.

Deano raised his fist to smash it into Liam's body. Liam dodged his first attempt. With his whole body, he slammed into Deano, forcing him backwards. If he could get a clear way to the door, he could grab Marco and get away.

But Deano was far stronger than Liam and he shoved back, sending him careening against the snooker table.

Out of the corner of his eye, Liam saw a bottle of whisky on the bar. He grabbed it and sent it flying towards Deano. It hit him straight in the face with a sickening thud.

Temporarily dazed, Deano swayed. Liam took his chance and jabbed a snooker cue hard into Deano's side, making him cry out in pain.

"You bastard," Deano screeched, his legs buckling underneath him.

Liam grabbed a snooker ball and, holding it in his palm, smacked Deano hard on the skull. Deano collapsed to the floor, giving Liam chance to break free.

Steve and Marco were still grappling at the foot of the stairs. Liam pulled Steve off, still kicking and screaming. Marco took the opportunity to land a hard punch in Steve's stomach, making him double over.

"Run," Marco shouted.

They got out of the pool house and ran straight into Jonny with three other lads Liam didn't recognise.

"Liam Moseley and his foreign bit of arse. What a treat to have you back here so soon," Jonny said with that cruel grin on his face.

"Fuck off, Jonny," Liam shouted. "I mean it. You don't know what you're dealing with."

Jonny didn't seem the least bit fazed by Liam's threats. He walked forward, as calmly as if he were in church. "I know exactly what I'm dealing with," he replied. "Some little queer who's got ideas above his station."

Marco stood in between Jonny and Liam. "You go through me first."

Jonny raised his hand. In it, he held a gun. "That would be a pleasure. I'll admit, I was a bit impressed that you got away from me once. A second time isn't acceptable though. You've pushed your luck way too far now."

He grabbed Marco by the hair. Two of the lads grabbed Liam. They were trembling more than him. They were way out of their depth.

"Get them inside," Jonny ordered.

In the snooker room, Deano stood, leaning on the snooker table for support. Steve struggled to his feet when he saw Jonny come in.

"You two are fucking useless," Jonny said. "I have to do everything."

He turned to another new lad who seemed absolutely terrified. "You. Get the stove on in the kitchen. Get some water to boil."

The lad—who must have been only nineteen—ran into the kitchenette to carry out Jonny's orders. Liam and Marco were stood up against the wall, hardly daring to move.

"This has been fun, but you're starting to seriously impact my business now," Jonny snarled. "Fucking stupid to show up at my house. Did you think your little decoy would leave me vulnerable?"

Liam looked at Marco, who stared absolute daggers at Jonny. If Liam could get Marco free to unleash that rage, they might have a chance. He prayed that Claire had the engine running.

"The games stop here," Jonny continued, moving to Marco. "I'm going to burn every last bit of skin I can find on both of you unless you tell me who the fuck you're working for. If you do that for me, I promise I'll make it quick. It's a tough choice, lads, but you're forcing my hand."

"How many pans, Jon?" the lad shouted through from the kitchen.

"Jesus Christ," Jonny screamed back. "All of them. It's not a Gordon Ramsay cooking demonstration, is it?"

More clattering came from the kitchen. Who would Jonny pick first? Either way it would be torture for the other. Then an idea, a misdirection snaked into his mind. Would it work? Only one way to find out... "His father landed last night," Liam blurted out.

Jonny stopped and stared. "His *father*?"

"Some big guy from Sicily. I'll ring them. Set up a meet," Liam stammered.

This time he did glance at Marco who looked at him wide-eyed.

"You?" Jonny said.

"Yeah me. They'll pay for him. He's family," Liam continued. "Don't you want to meet the organ grinder, Jon?"

"A father, eh?" Jonny said, deep in thought. "That puts a different spin on it. You're right. Whoever the fuck you work for might pay. Where were these brains when you worked for me? Go on then, clever lad. Call them."

Liam rifled in his pocket and dialled the number for the burner phone they had bought Claire at the services. They didn't trust her phone—it had been supplied by Jonny.

"Hi, it's me. Yeah, mission failed. Jonny has us. He says he'll kill us if you don't show up. His place. As soon as you can, yeah?" Liam terminated the call and stared at Jonny. "They're on their way."

"It's good to have family," Jonny said to Marco. "Thing is, this little bag of shit doesn't have fuck all. Either way, it won't affect your price if we try and get some information out of him."

"Take him in the kitchen," Jonny said to the two lads. "Deano. Steve. Keep our foreign friend entertained."

"No." Marco shouted, but a recovered Deano punched him square in the face.

"Shut the fuck up," Deano snarled.

The two lads dragged Liam kicking and screaming into the kitchenette. To his horror four pans were full of water that had begun to boil.

"First we'll try your left hand," Jonny said. "Then your right. Don't worry, handsome, your head will be the last bit of you."

Liam struggled with all his might, but they had him in a tight grip. Deano forced his way past him so he stood next to the cooker.

"Let me have a go," he said with a grin. "This little poof has been pushing me for months."

Jonny had gone that shade of red again. Would it be too much to ask for him to die of a heart attack immediately? "I told you to stay in there with Steve," he shouted.

"Don't worry—"

But Deano never got chance to finish his sentence. A huge crash had them yanking their heads towards the sound—and Marco appeared in the doorway, clutching bottles of spirits. He threw them, one after the other, into the kitchen.

A bottle of gin smashed against the wall, sending shards of glass raining down on Jonny and Deano. A bottle of brandy ricocheted off one of the lads holding Liam. It too shattered on the floor. With all the strength he could muster, Liam hooked his foot under the lad's ankle and sent him falling to the ground.

A bottle of rum smashed against the cooker canopy and spilled onto the hob. The alcohol hit the gas, sending flames licking across the countertop. They soon caught up with the gin dripping down the walls and the brandy on the floor—the kitchen went up in flames.

Liam broke free and forced his way out of the pool house. He filled his lungs with the clean air as he got outside. Marco was by his side. The others were spilling out of the pool house too, dragging a dazed Deano.

"Come on," Liam cried.

A gunshot sounded, making everyone freeze.

Jonny trained the gun on them both.

"You know what? I don't actually give a fuck anymore," Jonny snarled. "I just want you two dead."

Liam braced himself. Jonny would shoot him last. He would get a kick out of him seeing Marco felled.

In the corner of his eye, he could see the flames taking hold in the kitchen and spreading through into the snooker room.

Suddenly a car sped up the drive. It was Claire, but Jonny didn't know that.

"You're fucked now," Liam said.

Jonny dithered for a second, giving Marco just enough time to get the last bottle of lighter fluid out of his open bag. He threw it into the pool house where it exploded, sending flames everywhere. The trail of fluid they must have left on the stairs ignited and the attic lit up.

It all happened in a second. Jonny had just trained the gun on Liam and Marco when a blood-curdling scream rang out. "Sadie?" Jonny shouted, genuine fear gripping his face.

"You've got a choice now, fucker," Marco shouted.

"Fuck you," Jonny shouted back.

He raised the gun to shoot Marco at point-blank range. Before he knew what he was doing, Liam leapt in front of Marco.

A bang almost deafened him, and a heavy weight slamming into the top of his chest knocked the breath out of him.

Then he had a sense of falling. Jonny raced to the pool house and the young lads were running in all directions.

He hit the ground with a thud. Breathing was becoming harder.

It all got very confusing. Marco and Claire stood over him, their hands all over his body.

He needed to sleep. That would fix it all.

He closed his eyes and let the darkness envelop him.

Chapter Twenty-Three

Two weeks later

The car rattled on the rough old farm track. Liam winced. He might have had the stitches out, but his stomach was still tender. "Can't you take it easy?" he grumbled.

"Sorry," Claire replied. "You can take it up with the bloody landlord. Two old brothers lived in it until three years ago and it's been empty ever since. Let's say it needs a bit of TLC."

At last they reached the top of the hill and the valley stretched out before them. In the distance, the hazy skyscrapers of the Manchester skyline reached up to the skies. "I guess it's good to be out of the city," he managed.

"We can make it lovely." Claire put her hand on his leg. "I thought I'd lost you, Li, when I saw you go down like that."

Liam rested his hand on top of hers. "Let's not think about it."

Claire pulled up in the old farmyard and led Liam into the house. The anticipation was killing him. Where was Marco? The thought of seeing him again was making him excited and nervous in one big energy ball.

"Hello?" she called out.

Shaun appeared in the doorway. He threw his arms around Liam, who cried out.

"Steady. I'm a bit sore yet."

Standing back, Shaun frowned, looking Liam up and down. "Are you sure you should be out? When I spoke to the doctor yesterday, they said you could do with another week."

He'd been lucky. The bullet had grazed his liver and lodged in some muscle tissue. "They said it was my choice. I wanted to be here. I can't sleep in those places. I can't sleep until I've found a bit of peace, Shaun."

His brother nodded. "Fair enough."

Two heavyset men came out of the room.

"Liam, this is Enzo and this is Giovanni," Claire said.

Liam shook both their hands. They could almost be twins except Giovanni had silver hair and Enzo the same dark brown as Marco.

"At last, some back-up, eh?" Liam said.

"You should have waited for us," Enzo said.

Liam nodded. "I know that now. Where is he?"

Enzo glanced at Giovanni before turning to Liam. "Round the side of the house. There's a garden. He's waiting in there. He said he didn't want us all gawping when you saw each other."

"The dramatic scene is set." Liam laughed. "I might have known."

When Shaun had told him that Marco couldn't come to the hospital, Liam had been angry. He hadn't seen him since that moment at Jonny's. Having Claire and Shaun had been wonderful but he craved Marco's touch. He understood, but it didn't make it any easier.

"Will you be all right?" Claire asked.

Even though he had no idea, Liam nodded and made his way outside. The view from the farmyard was spectacular but he couldn't stop and admire it now. If this dragged on, he would have plenty of opportunity in the future.

He followed the old stone walls to the end of the building and went round the corner. A little garden with fruit trees was against the side of the house. At the end someone had put a bench, and on that bench sat Marco Ponti.

It might only have been a fortnight but Liam's whole body came alive when he saw him. Two weeks of being penned-up in that ward and all he could think about was this man. Marco looked up and they locked eyes.

Despite his injuries, Liam ran to the bench. Marco had stood by the time he got there and they flung their arms around each other.

"It's so good to see you," Marco said. "I've been going out of my mind."

They broke the embrace and Marco guided him to the bench.

"You have? Try two weeks of some old duffer farting morning, noon and night in the next bed." Liam shuddered at the memory.

Taking hold of Liam's hand, Marco kissed him. "You took a bullet for me," he said. "I can't believe it."

Liam squeezed his hand. "I told you I wouldn't let anyone hurt you again."

"Does this mean…"

Once again that hopeful and leg-melting smile appeared on Marco's face. Did he do this on purpose?

"I've got a deal for you, Marco Ponti."

"I'm listening."

"What you said in the bushes at Jonny's. That you love me. Did you mean it?"

Marco nodded.

Liam sighed. "It looks like I love you too, doesn't it? Otherwise I wouldn't have thrown my bloody body in front of that mad bastard—"

He couldn't finish what he said as Marco kissed him. Running his fingers through Marco's soft curls and tasting his tongue in his mouth was perfection. Marco rested his hand on Liam's thighs.

"Isn't there usually a bear hug attached to your kisses?" Liam questioned.

"I don't want to hurt you," Marco confessed.

"Put your bloody arms around me," Liam instructed.

They resumed the kiss and this time Marco pulled him close. The smell of him filled Liam's nostrils. This was what he wanted—every sense to be taken up with Marco Ponti.

Eventually they broke apart and Marco looked him in the eyes. "Forever?"

"Forever is a long time," Liam replied.

"Not in our game," Marco said. "Jonny is still out there."

When he'd been in the hospital, Liam had forbidden Claire or Shaun from even mentioning the name. The police had been all over them when he'd been brought in. They had agreed to say that the gun had gone off by accident and they were all friends. There was still honour amongst thieves.

"Speaking of him. What's the latest?"

They settled on the bench, Marco with his arms slung around Liam's shoulders.

"Missing in action. Once they dragged Sadie out of the pool house, she had been burnt pretty good."

Her screams had filled Liam's nightmares.

"Is she alive?"

Marco nodded. "But they've all disappeared. Jonny, Harry, Deano. The house is boarded up."

Liam frowned. "He wouldn't run. Not Jonny Wellingham."

"Maybe he shit himself at the thought of my Sicilian father?"

Liam knew that to be wishful thinking. Jonny would be apoplectic that they had got one over on him.

"And the city?"

"Running like clockwork," Marco said. "Your little friend has the girls under her control and I paid Jonny's debts off."

"You did?" Liam couldn't understand why on earth Marco had done this.

"I did. I want Manchester to be seen as a stable market again. We've taken his supply lines now."

Cuddling into Marco, it was clear. "You're a wily bastard."

"I don't know what that means, but I like it."

"You know he'll come back, don't you?"

A bird called to another bird, high above the little orchard that they sat in.

"My uncle will be here soon."

"He takes his bloody time, doesn't he?"

"He doesn't want to show his face until he's ready. Plus he's training up a whole new squad of men. Six months and they'll be here."

Liam looked up. "Six months? What are we supposed to do until then?"

Marco kissed his hand. "We run this city like it's supposed to be run and…"

"And?"

"We fall deeper in love. Can you handle that?"

Liam leant forward and kissed him. "I can handle it."

Liam settled happily into Marco's arms and stared down the valley. The streets of Manchester could be a million miles away. But they weren't. It gave Liam chills that they could be calling the shots. He had never dreamt about it before. "I think we can do this, you know," he said, quietly.

Marco took hold of his hand, kissing the back of it. "I think we can do anything if we do it together. Please don't go taking stupid risks again. I can't lose you, Liam."

The look in his eyes humbled Liam.

"We've been running all this time. Now we have power," he said. "I won't leave you again, Marco. I love you."

Want to see more from this author? Here's a taster for you to enjoy!

Two Tribes: Everything Changes
Kristian Parker

Excerpt

A mechanical reindeer serenaded the city with a rendition of *Away in A Manger.* It was like a call to arms for crowds of people who flocked to Manchester's centre to stand out in the freezing cold, getting drunk on overpriced beer. All in the name of celebrating the festive period.

The smells of cinnamon and hot dogs competed as Shaun Moseley walked through the packed crowds. He had woken up to the wonder of Christmas late in life. His upbringing had been a long way from the perfect families he had watched with envy on the television. His mother thought good parenting had been to let them sit in the pub with her and her mates instead of leaving them at home. Shaun had preferred to stay at home. At least then his younger brother, Liam, could fall asleep in his own bed instead of a pub floor.

Even with those thoughts milling around in his head, the cheer bursting out of Manchester this drizzly afternoon was infectious. He got his mobile phone out of his jacket and dialled.

"If you're ringing to tell me we're not having curry for dinner tonight, I'm going to be upset."

Typical of Liam. No hello or anything. Straight to what he'd be fed that night. He didn't deserve to be so slim.

"Have no fear, I've already made it," Shaun grumbled. "Bloody hell, do you always think with your stomach?"

"No," Liam replied with a laugh. "Ask Marco."

"Shut up. How gross."

"You're only jealous."

Talk about an understatement. "Too bloody right I am," Shaun muttered. "Three months without any action is like being in lockdown all over again. It's not natural."

"It must be hard," Liam said before collapsing into hysterics at his own joke.

"Hilarious," Shaun replied drily.

He walked deeper into the markets. It might have only been midday but already people were the worse for wear. Manchester had earned a reputation for hard partying many decades ago and the city still wore it as a badge of honour. It gave Shaun a strange sense of pride in his birth town. After being away for years, he had enjoyed spending the last few months here. Well, on the outskirts, but he took trips into town whenever he could.

The stalls were packed with things. Food, cooking implements and, for some reason, bird tables. Shaun could just imagine a husband leaving his Christmas gift shopping until the last minute and panic-buying one. He had no idea how one of those things would be wrapped.

"So, what did you want? Not to ask about my sex life, I'm sure," Liam continued.

"Nothing much. I'm in the markets and it made me feel all Christmassy," Shaun replied. He stopped and examined a stuffed robin in a waistcoat. Who on earth would buy that?

"It's bloody weeks away yet," Liam moaned. "I haven't even thought what to get Marco. It's a bit hard when he won't let me out of his sight."

He had a point. Ever since Liam had been released from hospital after being shot by crime boss Jonny Wellingham, Liam's boyfriend Marco Ponti hadn't let him move without being by his side. That would drive Shaun mad, but Liam was in love and lapped it up.

Careful, Shaun, you're beginning to sound like a jaded old queen.

"They've invented a new thing, little brother," Shaun said. "It's called the internet. I'll show you when I get home. It's brilliant."

"Funny guy," Liam replied. "You're as bad as him, anyway. You've only been gone an hour and you're checking up on me."

Bored of the stuffed animals, Shaun moved on to a stall that had a revolutionary garlic press whose sign proclaimed he'd been living half a life without. Shaun examined it and wasn't sure that was strictly true. He'd managed for over thirty years without this essential piece of kit. He had an inkling he could struggle on for the rest.

"Actually, it wasn't about you, believe it or not. I wanted to talk to you about Christmas," he said. "I might go home to Blackpool. It would be nice to see some of the guys." Silence on the other end of the line told him what Liam thought of that idea. "Liam? Are you still there?"

"You know you can't," Liam said quietly. "Marco said it isn't safe yet."

Shaun slammed the garlic press back down onto the stall.

"Breakages are paid for," said the stall holder.

It was hard to take someone seriously who had garlic bulb earrings with a matching necklace.

"Sorry," he mouthed to her. But the ever-present frustration had risen up in him. "Fuck's sake, Liam. It's been three months. Wellingham is probably on the Costa del Knobhead, drinking sangria or something."

Liam sighed. "Until their uncle comes and gets things properly running, you can't. It won't be for much longer. Besides—"

"Besides what?" Shaun snapped.

"I thought it might be nice for us to spend it together," Liam said shyly. "It's been years."

A flash of guilt replaced the anger. They hadn't had Christmas together since Shaun had left Manchester many years ago. He'd been travelling too much. Then when he went to Blackpool, Liam had taken up with Wellingham's gang and couldn't be persuaded to come to his. Shaun had found it hard to tempt him to a nut roast in a yoga bed and breakfast when Jonny offered drink, drugs and God knew what in a mansion.

"I suppose I'm cooking the dinner as well, am I?" Shaun asked.

"It will give you something to think about," Liam answered. "You love planning shit like this. Remember your thirtieth? You choreographed your own surprise party."

Shaun couldn't deny it. He didn't like to leave things to chance. "So we'll all sit around eating turkey and Christmas pud?" he asked.

"Don't forget the crackers."

"Like one big happy family, eh?"

"You could make an effort, seeing as it's Christmas," Liam offered.

"I will talk to you, Dolly and Claire," Shaun said haughtily. "Maybe Marco if he doesn't keep banging on about being a big gangster."

"Fine, whatever," Liam said.

Shaun could hear himself being mean — a frequent occurrence since he'd been caught up in this whole nightmare. Staying by Liam's bedside those awful days in the hospital, he'd vowed to take better care of his brother. Now he was being childish because he couldn't go to his mates at Christmas. They still thought he was looking after Liam so it wasn't like they even expected him.

"Well, I suppose I'd better get the rest of my shopping done. I thought I'd do those homemade naans you like."

"Ace. I'll tell Marco, he loves them. Oh and, Shaun…"

"What now?" Shaun laughed. "You're very needy today, Li."

"Remember that fudge stall on Brazenose Street? I wonder if it's still there."

When their mother would spend the afternoon in the pub, she would give them a ten-pound note to spend on the markets. Shaun would always go straight for chocolate, but Liam plumped for as much fudge as he could buy. Then he would nibble his collection every day to make it last. Of course, Shaun's chocolate would be gone before the Queen made her speech.

"I reckon it will be," Shaun said with a smile.

"Pretty please," Liam begged.

Shaun sighed. "You soft lad. It's miles back the way I've just come from."

"Pretty please with cherries on top?"

How could he refuse him? Liam had missed out on so much in his short life and even though Wellingham's bullet had nearly killed him, he was happier than Shaun had ever seen him.

"Fine, seeing as it's you," Shaun said. "But I get to choose the flavours. You always had weird shit like cherry fizz or lemon meringue."

"I only did that to keep you off them," Liam confided.

"Crafty little shit."

Shaun set off the way he had just been. In doing so, he walked straight into an incredibly good-looking young man behind him. But that wasn't what made Shaun jump. Keeping as calm as possible, he pushed past and set off towards the edge of the market, his heart racing.

"I'll let you go then," Liam said with a chuckle.

"Wait," Shaun said, unease flooding his system. "I don't know if I'm being paranoid, but I think someone's following me."

"What? Tell me what you mean," Liam said. All traces of amusement had left Liam's voice.

"This guy. I saw him in Marks and Spencer and in the food market. Now I've just headed back to that bloody fudge stall and he's there. Right behind me."

"Are you sure it's the same person?" Liam replied.

"Course I am. He's gorgeous. I never forget a fit lad. Like I said, I'm probably just being paranoid. Manchester isn't all that big."

He wasn't sure if his mind was playing tricks on him, but it felt like the crowds had become denser. Office workers still in their formal clothes but with flashing antlers on their heads shouted to one another over the din. Shaun wanted to fight his way to the street now. He glanced back and to his horror, the guy wasn't far behind him.

"Okay, I'm not being paranoid. He's following me. Absolutely sure of it," he whispered. He half expected a hand to grab his shoulder at any moment. He might be surrounded by people, but Shaun could hardly beg a stranger for help.

"Act natural. I'll dial Marco in," Liam said.

Shaun wanted to run, but they had rehearsed this so many times he remembered what Marco had drilled into him. *Don't give away that you know. If you panic, they will panic, then things can get out of hand.*

With every bit of his self-control, he walked slowly past the little wooden chalets selling their wares as though he were browsing like anyone else.

"Shaun?"

Marco Ponti had the thickest Italian accent to go with his brooding good looks. If he hadn't been an ambitious gangster who'd nearly got them killed, Shaun would have been happy for his brother. But now Shaun needed his confidence and knowledge.

"What do I do?" Shaun replied.

"Stay calm. Can you get a photo?" Marco asked.

Shaun frantically scanned the markets. He saw a man dressed as an elf, giving out free chocolates. He dashed over.

"Any chance of a pic?" he asked him. "My brother is after an outfit like this for Christmas morning. I said I'd make him one."

The man nodded and Shaun made a big fuss of positioning himself to get the selfie absolutely perfect. He managed to get the mysterious figure in one of them and sent it off to Marco.

"You have a happy Christmas," Shaun said to the elf and carried on towards the street.

He tried to work out the best escape routes out of the city. He'd got the train in from the little village near their old farmhouse hideout. The last thing he wanted was to lead any would-be attackers there. He had to lose them somehow.

"Did you get it?" he asked.

"Just looking," Liam said. "Shit, fuck. It's Deano."

Terror gripped Shaun. Deano was the worst of Wellingham's henchmen. He'd hated Liam when they had both been in the gang together. Him along with the rest of Wellingham's Boys had been on the missing list ever since Marco had burned Jonny's pool house to the ground. Shaun had been sure that Jonny would cut his losses and leave town. He'd been wrong.

"Okay, Claire has been on to Giovanni and Enzo. Giovanni is miles away, but Enzo is only in Moston. He'll be at Aldi in Ancoats in twenty minutes. Can you get there?"

Enzo and Giovanni were Marco's muscle-bound cousins. Exceptionally handsome but constantly preoccupied with pumping iron, Shaun had given them a wide berth ever since they'd arrived.

"Ancoats is fucking miles away."

"I know, but if he comes any farther in, he'll get caught up in traffic. Can you do it?" Marco asked.

Shaun glanced around again. Every young man could be a potential attacker.

"I'm scared, Marco," he said quietly.

"Listen to me. You have to keep up the pretence. You're just on a shopping trip. Laugh."

"What?"

"Laugh. I've just told you the best joke ever. You have no cares in the world. Fucking laugh."

Shaun did as he was told, he wouldn't have won an award for his performance, but it would do. "I'm nearly at the street. Then what?"

"Stop and browse at the stall next to you. You're in no rush, remember."

Shaun found himself showing an interest in an apple-shaped wine cooler. The hopeful stall holder approached.

"Once I get to the street, what do I do?" Shaun asked, ignoring the man who seemed determined to impress him with a demonstration on how to get the top of the cooler off.

"Get to the Northern Quarter," Liam said. "It'll be crowded."

A bead of sweat trickled down Shaun's back even though the December air had chilled him all day.

"I'm not cut out for this. I don't think I can—"

Panic rose within him. He'd been sure he wouldn't be affected by this life. He'd refused to have anything to do with their dodgy deals ever since Liam, Marco and the others had turned up on his doorstep in Blackpool. Shaun had accused Marco of being paranoid for making him stay with them all these weeks. He'd only done it so Liam would focus on getting well again.

"Shaun," Marco barked down the phone. "You have no choice. Get yourself ready. Swallow it down and do everything I tell you."

Shaun tried to control his panic and fought the temptation to lay into Marco. None of them would be in this position if he'd just done what his uncle said and waited for reinforcements from Italy. Instead, he'd taken it upon himself to try and ruin Jonny Wellingham. That had resulted in Liam taking a bullet and Shaun being trapped with the rest of them. Jonny evidently did see him as a target and now he needed Marco to get him out of there alive. "Okay, ready," he managed.

"Then go."

Shaun wandered to the edge of the market. Crowds were spilling out onto the pavements and tired security guards kept telling them to get back in with their drinks. Shaun desperately wanted to throw himself on their mercy and beg for help, but that would only cause bigger issues further down the line. He had no appetite for being labelled a grass on top of everything else.

"Tell Enzo he'd better bloody be there," Shaun said.

"He will be, and I'll be on the other end of the phone all the time. You can do this, Shaun," Marco coaxed.

Summoning all this inner strength, Shaun stepped out of the seemingly safe confines of the markets. He'd been on the pavement mere seconds when a car roared up from a side street. It screeched to a halt metres from where he stood.

To his horror, Deano grabbed hold of his arm and hauled him towards the car. Shaun heard Marco calling his name down the phone, but it all happened so quickly.

The rear door of the car opened, and Jonny Wellingham's long-time deputy, Harry, glared at him from the back. There were no prizes for guessing who would be at the other end of this joyride. If he got in that vehicle, his life might very well be over.

Then the rage built within him. He would not die like this. He had escaped these bastards once in his life. He would do it again.

There were plenty of people around to witness what was going on. Surely he could use that to his advantage. Then a sharp stab of pain stung in his side, telling him that this Deano had a knife to him.

"If you say anything, I'll stick you," Deano whispered in his ear.

But Shaun wasn't going to be scared that easily. "Help," he screamed. "This man is trying to rob me. He's got a knife."

The security who had been dealing with unruly drinkers spun around. A young couple stood open-mouthed.

Deano slapped him on the shoulder. "Come on, Shaun. These people won't know you're joking. Sorry, he gets a bit confused when he's had one too many."

To Shaun's relief, Deano released his grip ever so slightly.

"Get him in the fucking car," Harry shouted.

Deano jabbed the knife harder.

Shaun didn't fancy bleeding to death while day trippers took selfies with him. "Help me," he screamed. Shaun wriggled out of Deano's clutches, exposing the knife. A woman screamed when she saw it.

The security guards were approaching at speed now. Shaun could see one talking into his headset. He prayed it would be to the police. Deano pulled the blade away from him. Relief flooded through Shaun's body, making his legs turn to jelly. But now wasn't the time to lose it, not when he was a long way from safety.

Two lads were getting out of the car, but before they could do anything, Shaun shoved Deano with all his might. He fell against a handmade candle stall. The stall tipped over, sending hundreds of candles in all the colours of the rainbow rolling along the floor. The stallholder shouted and grabbed hold of Deano, who was trying to get up. Shaun saw his opportunity.

He ran as fast as his legs would carry him out of the markets and into the main shopping streets of the city. When he reached the corner, he glanced back to see lads scrambling out of the car. One hollered when they saw him.

The chase of Shaun's life was on.

About the Author

I have written for as long as I could write. In fact, before, when I would dictate to my auntie. I love to read, and I love to create worlds and characters.

I live in the English countryside. When I'm not writing, I like to get out there and think through the next scenario I'm going to throw my characters into.

Inspiration can be found anywhere, on a train, in a restaurant or in an office. I am always in search of the next character to find love in one of my stories. In a world of apps and online dating, it is important to remember love can be found when you least expect it.

Kristian loves to hear from readers. You can find his contact information, website details and author profile page at https://www.pride-publishing.com

PUBLISHING

Sign up for our newsletter and find out about all our
romance book releases, eBook sales and promotions,
sneak peeks and FREE romance books!